"I don't want to date or be friends. But I wouldn't mind sleeping with you again."

He went silent on the other end.

"Dash?" I doubled-checked. "Are you still there?"

"Yeah, I just... Tracy, are you asking me for a one-night stand?"

"I'm asking you to have an affair. But I have some rules you'll have to agree to."

"Let's hear them."

"First, you can't sleep with anyone except me while we're together. Second, no going out in public. Third, no buying me things. Fourth, I'm not recording a duet with you. And last, we walk away clean when it's over."

"Damn, Tracy. You're really methodical about this."

"Are you interested or should I just hang up?"

"Can I impose some rules, too?"

"No."

"Can we at least try to make it seem like a date?"

"It won't change anything. It'll still just be sex." She couldn't be tempted to want more.

* * *

Wild Nashville Ways by Sheri WhiteFeather is part of the Daughters of Country series.

Dear Reader,

Sometimes life is hard. I've had a tough time these past few years with family illnesses and emotional issues. But it helps to keep busy, and writing *Wild Nashville Ways* kept me occupied.

Dash and Tracy, the hero and heroine of this story, are struggling with family issues, too. But there's always hope, and their love affair keeps them busy. Wonderfully, wildly busy—in each other's arms.

There's nothing like a sexy romp (or a romantic book) to keep your mind off your troubles.

Love and hugs,

Sheri WhiteFeather

SHERI
WHITEFEATHER

WILD NASHVILLE WAYS

Recycling programs for this product may not exist in your area.

ISBN-13: 978-1-335-20923-8

Wild Nashville Ways

Copyright © 2020 by Sheree Henry-Whitefeather

Harlequin Enterprises ULC
22 Adelaide St. West, 40th Floor
Toronto, Ontario M5H 4E3, Canada
www.Harlequin.com

Printed in U.S.A.

Sheri WhiteFeather is an award-winning bestselling author. She lives in Southern California and enjoys shopping in vintage stores and visiting art galleries and museums. She is known for incorporating Native American elements into her books and has two grown children who are tribally enrolled members of the Muscogee Creek Nation. Visit her website at www.sheriwhitefeather.com.

Books by Sheri WhiteFeather

Harlequin Desire

Sons of Country

Wrangling the Rich Rancher
Nashville Rebel
Nashville Secrets

Daughters of Country

Hot Nashville Nights
Wild Nashville Ways

Visit her Author Profile page at Harlequin.com, or www.sheriwhitefeather.com, for more titles.

You can also find Sheri WhiteFeather on Facebook, along with other Harlequin Desire authors, at Facebook.com/harlequindesireauthors!

One

Tracy

I answered the door, only to find Dash Smith, the hottest new country star on the planet, standing on my daddy's front porch.

"Hey, Tracy," he said, much too softly, as I just stood there and stared. He was as handsome as ever, with those expressive brown eyes, the rigid jaw, that slightly crooked, bend-a-woman-to-his-will mouth. I couldn't tell how his hair was styled beneath his baseball cap, but I was familiar with the inky black color.

He used to be my fiancé, back when both of us were struggling to make it. My damaged heart would argue that, somewhere inside the pain, I was still in love with Dash. That might be true. But that didn't mean I wanted anything to do with him.

"What are you doing here?" I hoped he hadn't tracked me down at my father's house to bug me about working with him. We broke up nearly six years ago, and I'd done my best to heal, focusing on my music and moving on to other lovers. Then just this year, during the height of his success, he'd started texting me from his world tour, prodding me to do a duet with him when he returned. Call me stubborn, but I wasn't going to make a record with my ex, no matter how badly my flagging career needed the boost. Besides, this was *not* the day to discuss it.

He frowned. "Didn't your dad tell you? I'm going with you to his surgery. I'm going to help afterward, too."

I clutched the doorknob, using it as an anchor. "No, he didn't say anything about you…" I shouldn't be surprised by Dash's involvement, though. He and Pop had remained friends throughout the years, texting and calling and seeing each other when they could. And now Pop was battling testicular cancer and would be having an orchiectomy this morning.

A faraway look came into Dash's eyes, and I suspected that he was thinking about his own father, who'd died from lung cancer a few years after our relationship ended. I'd attended the funeral, paying my respects and offering my condolences. I'd always loved his dad. Dash obviously adored mine, too.

With a lump forming in my throat, I glanced past

him, taking inventory of the luxury SUV parked in the driveway. A broad-shouldered man sat behind the wheel. Considering how intently he watched us, he was probably a bodyguard doubling as a driver. Dash had grown up dirt-poor, and now he had millions of dollars and an army of people protecting him.

"Do you want to come in?" I asked. I couldn't go against my dad's wishes and block Dash from helping out. But damn, it hurt being this close to him again. His father's funeral was the last time we'd seen each other, apart from today. "Pop is still getting ready."

He followed me inside, leaving his driver in the car. "That's fine."

No, I thought, none of this was fine. Since Dash's recent rise to stardom, I'd become consumed with his fame, reading nearly every online article, concert review and gossip tidbit written about him. Sometimes I even checked to see if he had a girlfriend. He hadn't been linked to anyone, but he probably had enough groupies to keep him occupied.

During my short-lived brush with the limelight, groupies never chased me. A flutter of fans, yes. Hot men offering to fulfill my sexual whims… *I wish*.

For Dash, it was an entirely different story. His social media followers called themselves Dashers. Did his groupies have a cutesy little reference, too, for when they climbed into his bed to devour him? Maybe the Dine-and-Dashers?

He moved farther into the living room. "You did a nice job of fixing this place up."

"Thanks." I'd used some of the money I'd earned from my first album to help remodel the dusty old horse farm where I'd been raised. As for my own house, I was struggling to keep it afloat.

I wanted to revive my career, but not by riding Dash's coattails. A few gossip sites had named me as his long-ago fiancée, but no one seemed to care. Of course, if we did a duet, it might stir a deeper interest in our past. I had too many other issues to confront. Not just Pop's cancer and my financial problems, but things pertaining to my own health and the baby Dash and I should've had.

I put my hand against my stomach, remembering the ache associated with my miscarriage. The sadness. The loss.

"Are you okay?" he asked.

I blinked, realizing that I was spacing out in front of him. I lowered my hand. I couldn't tell him what I was thinking about. "It's just a lot to take in."

He roamed his gaze over me. "With your dad?"

"Yes." And everything else, too, I thought.

He shifted his stance, and I took a step back, not wanting to get too close. He stood tall and broodingly handsome. I was tall, too, and our bodies used to fit so perfectly together. But that wasn't something I should be remembering.

He said, "If you don't mind, I'd like for you and your dad to ride with me. I brought my best bodyguard along," he added, confirming who the man in the car was. "But some of my other security guys will be at the hospital, too. Mostly to keep the press at bay, in case they catch wind of me being there."

Good grief. I hadn't even considered the media. "What are you going to say if they do find out? Won't they wonder what you're doing at a cancer ward?"

"I'll just tell them the truth, that I accompanied a friend. But we're hoping to avoid that. The hospital is going to set aside a private waiting room for us. They already have a policy in place about celebrities and public figures. Their employees aren't allowed to ask for selfies or post anything on social media. If they do, they could lose their jobs. We can't do much about other patients or their friends or family, though. But my team has a plan in place that should eliminate me coming into contact with the public. We'll be doing everything we can to protect your dad's privacy, so you don't need to worry about that. I already discussed all of this with your pop."

Dash tucked the baseball cap lower on his head, and I assessed his ensemble. He wore indigo jeans and a pale-gray Western shirt, pricey sunglasses hooked in his front pocket. But even with the dark glasses and hat, he was still going to be recognizable. He'd become too famous not to notice. Every song on his debut album had been certified gold or higher, with some of them crossing over onto the pop charts.

"Are you sure my dad is okay with all of this?" I asked.

"He assured me that he was, but you can confirm it with him."

"I should probably check to see what's taking him so long, anyway." I also needed to get a grip on my emotions. How many years had I spent, wishing that Dash believed in love? He'd only asked me to marry him because of the baby, and that hurt as much now as it did back then.

I turned on my heel and walked down the narrow hallway, eager to get away from him. He'd admitted from the start that he thought love did more harm than good, and he wanted no part of it. I'd known that his feelings stemmed from his estranged mother and her abandonment of him and his dad, but I'd been foolish enough to think that I could fix what she'd broken.

I'd been motherless for a portion of my life, too. But mine hadn't run off. She died when I was in middle school, and Pop and I still missed her every day.

I knocked on his door, and he called out, "Come in!"

I inched my way inside and found him seated at his ancient rolltop desk. He was pulling on his boots.

With his graying hair and sun-weathered skin, he looked older than his fifty-nine years. He was a former rodeo cowboy, a bronc rider who'd never become as successful as he'd hoped. Of course, he was a horse breeder, too. But he'd also worked as a short-order cook when I was young, doing whatever was necessary to keep me in ribbons and bows, however tattered. As hard as he'd tried, we'd still been poor. But nothing like Dash. When he was a kid, they'd lived in a run-down trailer, going to food banks and collecting welfare in between his daddy's sporadic day jobs and music gigs.

"Is Dash here?" Pop asked.

"Yes." Only I needed to know what the deal was. "I don't understand why you asked him to do this."

"I didn't ask. He offered."

"To do what, exactly?"

"To keep you company at the hospital and to help with my recovery once I come back home, too. I thought it would be easier to have a man around, in case I get grossed out trying to change the bandages myself. It's not a good idea for you to do, either. That's just too personal for me."

As far as I knew, my father wasn't a squeamish guy. I'd seen him cut and bruised and climbing back in the saddle during his rodeo days. But maybe this was different. Or maybe he was making excuses.

I cautiously said, "I understand and accept that you and Dash have done your best to remain friends and keep in touch. But we could've talked to one of your old bronc riding buddies about coming by to help you with the bandages. It didn't have to be Dash."

"I know, but I thought having him around might benefit you, too." He finished putting on his boots. "That it might sway you into doing that duet with him. Honestly, hon, why not let him help you get your career back on track?"

"I appreciate you trying to look after me, but I'd rather make a comeback on my own."

"Yeah, but I hate seeing how hard you work. You shouldn't have to bust your butt, balancing two jobs and trying to sell your songs yourself. Not when Dash is at your disposal. You need to take advantage of his fame."

I heaved a sigh. Pop didn't know that I was going through a personal crisis and that being around Dash was going to make it more difficult for me. And I didn't plan to tell him, either.

He said, "I'm sorry if I blindsided you by inviting Dash to come with us. But I think it would be nice for you to become friends again. I don't remember you ever fighting or trashing each other, not even when you broke up."

Yes, we'd parted amicably. After my miscarriage, I'd made the agonizing decision to end our engagement, and Dash hadn't tried to stop me. He'd just let me go, the desolation of our lost child drifting between us.

But I couldn't obsess about that now. "Let's just work on getting you well, Pop." My ailing father was my priority. And if that meant spending time with Dash to give my father peace of mind, then that was what I would do.

Dash's driver/bodyguard, a big stoic dude named Zeke, kept the motor running as we pulled up to a side entrance reserved for hospital personnel. Another of Dash's security guys was waiting for us there.

Zeke used a magnetic key card to unlock the door and usher us inside, while the other security guy parked the car. We made it into the building without incident.

We separated from there, with me taking Pop to get him checked in and prepped for surgery. Once I was alone, I would meet Dash in the private waiting room. I was glad that he wasn't going to be with me every step of the way. It had been tough enough riding in the car with him, while he and my dad talked horses and music and everything except the fact that Dash and I used to be a couple. I suspected Zeke could tell how uncomfortable I was. Analyzing people was probably a significant part of his job.

After I got Pop settled in, I wandered over to a vending machine. I wondered what Dash would do if I waited in one of the open areas instead of joining him in the private room. Would he send Zeke off to look for me?

I scanned the items in the machine and chose a candy bar. I cursed and got Dash one, too. It used to be a favorite of his. I had no idea if he even ate sweets now.

All these years later, he'd become a stranger to me. Then again, he'd always been an enigma: a man who used to hold me tenderly in his arms, without setting much store by love.

I cleared my mind and got a third candy bar for

Zeke. I'd been taught to be polite. Maybe too polite? I reminded myself that I was doing this for my daddy. I didn't want to create any bad mojo today.

The private waiting room wasn't hard to find. Zeke stood outside the door, blocking anyone else from entering. He looked like a stone wall, dressed in a dark suit.

As I approached him, I gave him a chocolate bar. He tucked it into his jacket pocket, his lips curling into an itty-bitty smile. But his reaction didn't make him any less intimidating. If I ever got famous enough to have security, I was going to want someone like him on my side.

My success had been nothing compared to Dash's. But for me, it had still been pretty amazing. I understood why my father wanted that for me again. But being in this situation was torture. I was nervous about being alone with Dash.

Zeke opened the door, summoning me to his boss. Dash definitely had all the power. Men often did, in my estimation. It wasn't supposed to be that way in this day and age, but I'd just gotten trapped in a male-dominated situation. Unfortunately, my father was partially to blame. If he hadn't helped orchestrate this reunion, I wouldn't be in such close quarters with my ex.

The room was small, the decor beige and bland and generic. The door snapped shut behind me, courtesy of the bodyguard.

Dash glanced up, and I sucked in my breath. I

wanted to leave a chair between us, but I forged ahead and sat beside him, hating how easily he commanded my attention.

I extended the candy bar I got for him. "I don't know if you eat these anymore."

He accepted it. "My trainer had me on a strict diet and workout routine when I was on tour, but I can cheat a little now."

He did look exceptionally fit, but he'd always taken care of himself. When I'd first met him, he was stacking bales of hay at the feedstore where we both worked, and had arms and abs to die for. Eventually, we'd bonded over our musical aspirations. But in the beginning, I just wanted to get my hands on that rock-hard body.

Did I look the same to him, with my long brown hair, medium blue eyes and natural curves? Either way, I'd matured, and so had he. He'd turned thirty while he was on the road, and I would be twenty-eight next month.

"Do you want to share this?" He unwrapped the candy bar and offered me a bite.

"I have my own." I showed him the one I'd tucked into a side pouch of my purse. I removed it and joined him in the chocolate-and-nougat fest. "Did anyone approach you while I was gone?" I asked. "Or take your picture?"

He shook his head. "The corridor I used was blocked off, so I was the only one who had access to it." He gestured to a door on the other side of the room. "I came in that way. But it's locked now."

And Zeke was protecting the entrance I'd used. "Your team really had it figured out."

"It helped that the hospital was so accommodating. They're used to dealing with celebrities in this town. I'm not the first, and I won't be the last."

True, but at the moment, he was the prince of Nashville. Everyone wanted a piece of him. Before he got famous, I'd had my piece, night after night, naked in his bed. The memory left me hungering for sex. I hadn't been with anyone for at least six months. I doubted that Dash could make the same claim.

"What did they say about the surgery?" he asked, interrupting my wayward thoughts. "Are they going to come get us when it's over and talk to you about it?"

"Yes. They'll also decide if Pop should stay here overnight or come home today or if he'll need chemo or radiation afterward." It all felt so up in the air.

"I'm sorry he's going through this. And that you have to deal with it, too. I know how much he means to you."

Yes, he knew. I was aware that he'd shared the same kind of closeness with his father, too. He'd even inherited his dad's musical abilities. Kenny Smith should've been a star like his son. But he'd never progressed beyond coffee bars and shoddy night-club gigs.

"It's a shame your dad didn't get to see your success," I said. "He would've been so proud of you."

He nodded. "It's been bittersweet, climbing the charts without him."

"I wonder where your mom is and what she thinks of your celebrity status."

He scowled. "I have no idea, but I don't want to talk about her."

Clearly, it remained a sensitive subject. I couldn't blame him for that. And since she'd left her family for a tremendously wealthy man, maybe she didn't give a hoot about Dash's illustrious career.

But I certainly did. We used to daydream about winning Grammys and CMAs and every other accolade out there. Except he'd done it without me. He'd already collected all sorts of Best New Artist awards.

Was I being an idiot, turning down the duet? No, I thought. I was being strong and independent, refusing to put myself at the mercy of the man I used to love.

Or still loved. Or whatever.

My feelings for Dash never failed to confuse me. I could kiss him right now and probably melt girlishly in his lap. I finished my damned candy bar instead, eating the last few gooey bites.

He reached over and ran his thumb over the left corner of my lips, and I flinched something fierce.

"What are you doing?" I pulled away, afraid of how instantly aroused I got.

"You had a piece of chocolate…"

I rubbed the spot he'd touched. "Is it gone?"

"Yes. I already got it." He pressed his hands against his jeans. "I didn't mean to startle you."

We gazed uncomfortably at each other. I glanced away, hoping that he would start a new conversation. I couldn't think of a single thing to say. The awkward silence was deafening. Problem was, I sensed that he was feeling the sexual tension, too.

A few minutes passed before he said, "Your dad told me that you're working at the feedstore again, running the front counter like you used to."

Well, shoot, I thought. Not exactly a topic I wanted to discuss. But better than the carnal quiet, I supposed.

I replied, "It's just a few days a week to make some extra money. I work as a virtual assistant, too, for a company that hires VAs to schedule social media content for their clients."

"My management uses a service like that."

"A lot of companies do." My income as a VA sucked, though. The pay at the feedstore wasn't any better. To steer the talk away from me, I said, "I heard that you bought a mansion, out in the country somewhere."

"It's a great place. But I haven't spent much time there yet. It's been a whirlwind year, being on the road." He hesitated. "You should come by sometime and let me show you around."

Oh, sure, like I was going to pop over and say hello. "Have you invited my dad to see it?"

"Not yet. But I'd just gotten off tour when he told me that he was sick. I could tell how glad he was when I offered to help. I think he's worried that if something happens to him, you'll be all alone."

My heart clenched. "I have friends, people I see."

"Yes, but he's also hoping that his illness will inspire you to work with me. He wants your career to take off again."

"He already told me how he feels about that." And I didn't need to hear Dash repeat it.

"What about following through on our idea from the past? Remember how we used to say that someday we would do a special song together?"

"I haven't forgotten. But that was a different time, a different place, a different life." And I couldn't do it, not even for my cancer-stricken dad.

Dash sat back in his chair, broody as ever. "Let me know if you change your mind."

I didn't respond. He'd just removed his hat to run his fingers through his hair, and now I was analyzing how beautifully the strands fell into place. He wore it short on the sides and longer on top, in a stylish undercut.

"Are you dating anyone?" he asked suddenly.

I squinted at him. Was he seriously inquiring about my love life? Just the question alone served as a reminder of how lonely I'd become, intensifying my current hardships.

I steeled my heart and said, "Not at the moment. But there's been lots of men since you." I wasn't lying about that. I'd played the field, even if I hadn't done it lately.

A muscle pulsed in his jaw. He seemed jealous, but it served him right. If he'd loved me, we'd still be together.

He tossed his hat aside. "I've scored a lot, too."

"Of course, you have. Groupies galore."

He rolled his eyes. "As if that matters, with the way you used to chase me at the feedstore."

I could've smacked that smug look right off his face. "That's not the same as you having groupies now. You weren't even famous then."

"You still wanted me."

"You wanted me, too," I shot back.

"We both wanted each other." He leaned toward me, his dark gaze boring into mine. "Maybe we should kiss and see if it still feels the same."

Everything inside me erupted: the past, the present, my uncertain future. "Really? And what would that solve?"

"Nothing, except I think it would leave us both clamoring for more, like it did back then."

"I could kiss you without wanting more." Earlier I'd imagined melting in his lap, but I wasn't feeling weak or soppy now. My body had gone taut, my breathing shallow, and my anger was roiling. "I can control myself around you."

"Oh yeah?" he snapped. "Then prove it."

Screw him, I thought, while I stared him down. We'd barely ever fought before. Little tiffs here and there, but never anything major. I'd always suppressed my temper. But I refused to do that now.

I grabbed his shoulders and put my face next to his, nearly bumping his forehead with mine. It felt good to be mad, to let the pain come rushing out.

"Here's your proof," I murmured hotly against his mouth. I was going to kiss him as if the world was about to end, then *never*, *ever* do it again.

Two

Dash

Maximum velocity.

Tracy thrust her tongue into my mouth, and my heart slammed against my rib cage. She wasn't wasting a bit of time, and I relished the full-speed feeling.

She tasted of lust and anger and chocolate. A strange sort of eroticism. She'd kissed me all sorts of ways in the past, but never like this. I returned the favor, devouring her with my pent-up passion. I pulled her onto my lap, and she rubbed against my fly.

Was she punishing me for everything that had gone wrong between us? The hurt? The loss?

She moaned, and I steadied her on my lap. I was

hard beneath my jeans, ridiculously aroused. Being punished by her felt painfully good.

When she pulled back, we both caught our breaths.

"Did you get enough?" she asked, still straddling me and making me ache.

"No." I feared that I would never get enough, not when it came to her. She'd always been my sexual ideal. She used to be my dearest friend, too, and I didn't have many of those. "Kiss me some more."

She stared at me, stony, harsh, dead-on. "This is going to be the one and only time, so don't get used to it."

"Whatever you say." I wasn't going to argue, not while she was giving me a pulsating thrill.

She narrowed her pretty blue eyes. "Maybe I should just let you go find one of your groupies instead."

"I can't help that they chase me." Women wanted me because I was rich and famous. And yeah, I liked it. Fame was an aphrodisiac. Money, too. The bigger my financial portfolio, the stronger I felt. "You should sing with me, Tracy. We should make music together." I wanted to help revive her career. I needed to, I thought. After everything we'd been through, it was all I had to give her. A piece of my fame.

I touched her cheek, softly, slowly. She used to want a piece of my heart, but she looked as if she hated me now.

"Don't," she said.

"Don't what? Be nice?" I was still waiting for her to rekindle the fire. "You can bite me, if you want. You can draw blood."

"Maybe I will." She pushed my hand away from her cheek. "Just stop touching me like that."

She used to get sweet and dreamy when I was gentle with her. But she was different than before. Or maybe she was just different with me. "Did you let all of those other guys touch you in nice ways?" Were they allowed to take over where I'd left off?

Her voice sharpened. "That's none of your business."

I hated imagining her with other men. For some stupid reason, I'd assumed that she'd barely had any lovers since me.

She leaned forward, plundering my mouth once again. She didn't bite me, but her kiss was still brutal and filled with wrath.

I held her with an iron grip. I couldn't get those other men out of my mind. I suspected that was how Tracy felt about my groupies, too. We were both jealous, but that only made this hotter, somehow. Former lovers steeped in envy and locked in lust, I thought.

Unfortunately, it didn't last. This time, when she tore her mouth away from mine, she got up off my lap.

"I'm done with you," she said, standing to smooth her clothes, even though they weren't out of place.

I stood as well, and let out my breath. I needed

to walk off my arousal. I paced the room, feeling like a caged animal.

Being punished didn't feel so good now.

And neither did my shame from the past. When she'd gotten pregnant, I didn't have the means to support a wife and child, and I'd been scared out of my wits.

But still, I'd tried. I'd offered to marry her, to give that poor kid a name. Of course, it was all gone now. The baby we'd conceived, our mixed-up engagement, even the adoring way Tracy used to look at me.

I quit pacing and spun around to look at her, this former fiancée of mine. I'd never even bought her a ring. I could barely make my rent back then, let alone purchase a piece of jewelry. I could afford to give her a gigantic rock now. But I wasn't going to marry her or have another baby. I was only trying to influence her career, if she would let me.

"That wasn't my intention," I said.

"What, the kiss?" She bit down on her bottom lip. "Then why did you bait me to do it?"

"It was an impulse." I noticed that her lipstick was gone. Not even a glimmer of it remained. I wiped the back of my hand across my mouth in case some of it had gotten on me. "I lost control."

"Well, my control was just fine."

"With the way you rubbed all over me?" I stared at her. "Yeah, right."

She glowered back. "I was teaching you a lesson."

I looked her up and down. She had a beddable body, packed with curves. She had wholesome features, though. When she wasn't made up, she looked innocent. I'd always found that fascinating. It made her seem like a chameleon, sultry one day and soft the next. I patted my knee, offering to let her climb back onto my lap. "Want to teach me another one?"

She jerked her chin. "Go to hell, Dash."

"I've already been there." The day my mother left had been the worst kind of hell. And so was the day Tracy had broken up with me. My aversion to love didn't make me any less human. Or any less hurt.

She resumed her seat. "You should be apologizing."

I slumped into my chair and crammed my hat back onto my head. "For what?"

"Making things more difficult."

I grimaced, feeling like a heel. "You're right. I'm sorry." I should be comforting her through her dad's illness, not causing turmoil.

She didn't reply, so I kept talking, hoping to make amends and lighten her mood. "Remember the Christmas when both of our dads went caroling with us? Mine brought his eggnog along, and yours couldn't carry a tune. What a pair they were."

She relaxed a little. "That's the same night I cooked for everybody."

"Best holiday meal I ever had." Not just the food, but watching her in the kitchen, following her dad's

SHERI WHITEFEATHER   29

recipes. "It's nice that your old man taught you how
to baste a turkey."

"And yours taught you to make his special eggnog."

"I can still whip up a batch when I have to." I'd
spent this past Christmas on the road, and hosted a
party for the crew. But I hadn't made the eggnog.
The gathering had been catered.

She reached into her purse, retrieved her compact
and reapplied her lipstick. After that, she checked
the time on her phone. She seemed anxious for some
news.

"Did they say how long the surgery will take?"
I asked.

She put her phone away. "An hour, maybe two. I
guess it depends on how it goes."

I studied her in the overhead light: the glossy
pink lipstick, the way her long, thick hair cascaded
down her back. Did she still flip her head over to
blow-dry it? I used to like watching her get ready
in the mornings.

We'd lived together in my apartment—a big,
messy place above an old storage barn. Ratty as it
was, I'd chosen it because I could make noise and
practice my music there.

Only it was Tracy who'd gotten a record deal.
Soon after our engagement ended, her career flour-
ished. I was alone, night after night, feeling like a
failure, while she'd moved on to bigger and better
things. At the time, it had solidified my biggest fear.

Her making it, and me being left behind. But I'd had other insecurities during our relationship, too, especially when she'd gotten pregnant. I'd downright panicked about becoming a father, worrying about how I was going to help support our child.

She checked the time again. "I wish we'd hear something."

"Do you need anything?" I asked, as a surge of emotion flashed through my veins. Our son or daughter would've been around five now and probably starting kindergarten this year.

"What do you mean, anything?"

"Something from the cafeteria. Or maybe a cup of coffee. I can have someone from my team make a food or drink run."

She shook her head. "I'm good. But they can get something for you."

"I'm all right." I didn't want coffee. I wasn't hungry, either. "The candy bar was enough for me."

"For me, too." She glanced at my mouth.

Was she thinking about the chocolate we'd tasted on each other's lips? The kiss that shouldn't have happened? I wouldn't be forgetting it anytime soon.

We waited in silence, and within the hour, a quick knock sounded, then the door opened and Zeke poked his head inside.

"The surgeon is here," he said.

Tracy leaped up from her seat, and the doctor entered, still attired in his scrubs.

I stood as well, and he acknowledged both of us

with a formal nod. He appeared to be in his mid-forties, with black-rimmed glasses, graying temples and an easy smile.

Did that mean it was good news? Lord, I hoped so. I moved closer to Tracy, to hear what he had to say.

Thankfully, the cancer hadn't spread beyond the testicle. But nonetheless, Tracy's beloved pop would be monitored over the next ten years, getting physicals and blood tests every three months for the first year, and less often as time went on. CT scans would also be done, and if all of those tests showed no sign of cancer, he wouldn't need further treatment. If the cancer returned, then he would require radiation or chemotherapy.

I'd taken care of my dad when he'd gotten sick, but his treatments didn't work. He'd been having some respiratory problems that he'd ignored, and by the time he discovered it was lung cancer, he was already in an advanced stage. He'd passed away within months of his diagnosis.

The doctor finished talking to Tracy, bade both of us goodbye and left the waiting room. Her dad would be coming home today.

She turned toward me, looking as if she might burst into tears. I assumed it was from relief. I wanted to hold her, to let her cry in my arms, but I doubted that she would welcome my touch.

She composed herself and said, "We're going to

have to keep Pop from overexerting himself. You know how stubborn he can be."

I nodded. "How long are you going to stay with him?"

"For as long as he needs me."

"What about your work?"

"I'm taking some time off from the feedstore, but I can do my VA stuff from his house. I won't be losing that income." She furrowed her brow. "How often are you coming over to help?"

"I'm not driving back and forth. I'm staying there, too."

"Oh, my God." She gaped at me. "Seriously? There's not even an extra bedroom for you."

"I don't mind sleeping on the couch." I didn't have my own room when I was a kid, either. "Besides, your dad already invited me to stay for a couple of weeks. Or longer if necessary. It depends on how he feels."

She snapped her mouth shut. Clearly, she wasn't happy with the arrangements that had been made. But she was just going to have to grin and bear it.

She wasn't grinning now. And neither was I.

I couldn't seem to stop myself from stressing over the fact that I was still attracted to her. Or that, other than my runaway mother, she was the only woman who'd ever mattered to me.

While Tracy got her dad settled into bed back at his house, I stayed outside with Zeke to discuss

a few things. He wasn't just my best bodyguard.
Aside from the fact that he co-owned the personal
protection company he worked for, he was also my
security chief.

He lifted my suitcase from the back of the SUV
and said, "I'll have someone bring your truck by
later."

"Thanks. What about the security cameras?"

"It's done. I had them installed while we were at
the hospital."

He removed his phone and showed me the app
that would allow him and the rest of the team to
monitor the perimeters of this property, keeping an
eye out for the press or anyone else who might catch
wind of me being here. The last thing I wanted was
a persistent reporter or an overzealous fan hanging
around and impeding Tracy's dad's recovery. There
weren't any neighbors to speak of. The farm sat on
enough acreage to separate it from other houses, but
I was still concerned about strangers.

"I can download it on your phone, too," Zeke said.

"That would be great." Later I would teach Tracy's
dad how to operate it. After all of this was over, the
cameras would be moved into the barn. Tracy's dad
was excited about that. Cameras could be especially
helpful for monitoring a mare getting ready to foal.

I handed Zeke my phone, then stood back to study
him. He had a naturally tanned complexion, hair as
black as mine, and strong, broad features. He was
an interesting mix of Samoan, Caucasian and Choc-

taw. I had a little Choctaw blood from my mom's side, but mostly I was Anglo. Some of my classmates used to call me white trash, their taunts cutting me to the quick.

Tracy had mentioned my mom earlier, but I'd lied when I'd said that I didn't know her whereabouts. A few months back, I'd asked Zeke to investigate her. And according to what he'd uncovered, she was no longer with the man she'd run off with. She'd had numerous lovers over the years. At last count, she'd taken up with a retired architect in Mexico and was living a reclusive life in a house he'd built that overlooked the sea.

I had no idea if she even knew that I was a celebrity. My music wasn't popular in Mexico. Of course, there was a part of me that wanted her to know, and another part that didn't give a shit. I'd only had Zeke investigate her to satisfy my curiosity about where she was.

"Here you go," he said, interrupting my thoughts. He'd finished downloading the app.

He showed me how to use it, and once he was gone, I went inside and placed my bag in the living room.

Tracy appeared from around the corner, then eyed my suitcase as if it might explode.

"Don't worry," I said. "I'll keep my stuff out of the way."

She made a weary sound. "It would be a lot easier if you went home."

I sat on the sofa, the same cozy spot where I would be sleeping. "Just give me a chance, okay?" I planned on making myself as useful as possible.

She sighed and plopped down beside me. "Should we go over the instructions from the hospital?"

"Sure." I'd won the first round, but I knew the battle wasn't over. Tracy was still unnerved by my presence. "We can divvy up your pop's care."

She removed the paperwork from her purse and read it to herself. I waited for her to give me the condensed version.

She said, "He needs to get enough sleep to recover. But he also needs to walk each day. Just a little at first, then increase it each time. He's supposed to avoid strenuous activities for the first few weeks, and he won't be able to drive until the doctor says it's okay."

"I can take care of the horses for him." I had plenty of time to devote to the animals. "I don't have anything going on except this. My tour is over, and I'm not going back into the studio for a while. My schedule is clear."

"All right, then I'll administer Pop's medications," she said. "There are pain pills and antibiotics for him to take."

"What kind of stitches does he have? Are they going to need to be removed or will they dissolve?"

She checked the instructions. "They'll dissolve. He needs to keep the incision clean and dry and change the bandage once a day. He can take showers, but no baths for the first few weeks. He can use ice packs for swelling." She glanced up at me. "I'll make a copy of this for you."

"Thanks. I think we're going to make a good pair."

She refolded the paperwork. "We aren't a pair."

I ignored her remark and said, "It's going to be interesting sharing a bathroom with you again." Her dad had his own bathroom, so we wouldn't be infringing on his privacy. "You always took forever getting ready."

She frowned. "You never seemed to mind before."

Was she thinking about how I used to watch her do her hair and makeup? "You never minded hanging around when I got ready, either." Sometimes she used to come up behind me in the mirror and loosen the towel that was wrapped around my waist, when I was fresh from the shower and attempting to shave. I'd never really been a morning person, but I'd enjoyed every naughty nuance of Tracy seducing me bright and early.

I blinked, and she stood and moved away from me. Had she tapped into what I was I thinking?

"Pop's got some laundry that's been piling up," she said, preparing to rush off. "I'll make sure there are clean linens for you to use tonight, too."

Tracy left the room, and I grabbed a rodeo magazine off the coffee table and paged through it, giving myself something to do.

About twenty minutes later, after I'd pretty much read it cover to cover, my phone chimed with an incoming text. I checked the message. It was Zeke, asking me to call him. He'd included a code we'd devised that pertained to my mom.

Why was he texting me about her? He'd only just left here a short while ago. Besides, he'd already told me everything he knew about her.

So maybe he wanted to discuss one of my "other" moms? Unfortunately, the public knew that my mother had split when I was a kid. Someone from our old trailer park had sold that information to a tabloid, and now, every so often, there were women on social media claiming to be her. My cybersecurity team contacted Zeke whenever things like that cropped up, and he always checked it out.

I went outside to the backyard and called him back.

"Hey," he said, answering straight away. "I'm sorry to bother you so soon, but I stopped by the management office and picked up today's fan mail. And there was a letter that caught my attention."

Sometimes he liked to go through my snail mail himself, screening it randomly. Otherwise, it was opened by my administrative staff.

"Go on," I replied, urging him to continue.

"It was from someone who said that her name is Lola, and that she used to sing and dance for you and your daddy."

His words hit me hard and quick. My mother's name was Darleen, but she used to sing "Whatever Lola Wants" and twirl around, pretending to be that character. I'd even memorized the song when I was little. "Mom never sang and danced in front of anyone like that except me and my dad, and I never told anyone about it but you." I paused. "What do you think this means?"

"It could be a message from her. Or it could be an imposter. She could've shared the Lola story with someone else, and they could've written the letter."

"What else was in it, besides Lola dancing for me and my daddy?"

"She complimented your music and said that she was proud of you. She also said that she didn't want you to be mad at her."

"For what? Walking out on me?"

"She didn't specify. But I suspect that you'll be hearing from her again. Whoever it is."

"More cryptic notes?" I was already frazzled by this one. I didn't know which scenario was worse: an imposter or the real deal.

My stomach clenched. "Is there a return address?"

"No, but it's postmarked Los Angeles, with a red lipstick mark on the back of the envelope."

As if it had been sealed with a kiss? My stomach tightened again. That actually seemed like something my mom would do, but why would she be reaching out to me after all this time? She couldn't have known that I'd had Zeke search for her. He'd been highly discreet about that.

"Can DNA be extracted from lipstick?" I asked.

"I don't think so," he replied. "But I'm going to have it examined, anyway."

"What about the flap on the envelope itself?"

"Most are self-adhesive now, but if there was saliva involved and if it's a viable sample, the lab can compare it to your DNA for a familial match. I'll also have it tested for fingerprints, just in case the person who sent it is in the system. Your mother doesn't have a criminal record, but an imposter might."

"What a thing to have to think about."

"I know. I'm sorry. Do you want to see the letter before I have it tested?"

"No." I trusted Zeke to do his job.

He said, "I have an old friend who works for US Customs and Border Protection, so I can check with him to see if your mom returned to the States and what port of entry she might've used. Anyone in the Los Angeles area could've mailed that letter or even sent it at her request, but at least we'll know if she traveled recently or was in California herself. I'll inquire about her boyfriend, too."

"Do whatever you need to do."

He cleared his throat. "I'll have all of the snail mail forwarded to me from now on. I don't know how long it will take for my friend at Customs to get back to me, but I can try to put a rush on the lab tests."

"Thanks. I should go." Of all days for this to happen. I could barely breathe. If this was my mother, was she trying to cast one of her mind-bending charms over me, like she used to do when I was a kid? Fawning over me one minute and ignoring me the next?

I ended the call and returned to the house. Tracy sat at the kitchen table, sorting through her dad's medications and putting them in a case with the days of the week stamped on it. Apparently, she was on a break from the laundry.

She glanced up and asked, "Where were you?"

"I was in the backyard. Did you think that I'd gone home already?" I joked, making light of my actions and trying to keep her from suspecting anything was wrong.

She rolled her eyes. "I knew you had to be around somewhere."

Yes, I was around, standing right in front of her, faking a casual air. As overwhelming as it was, I would never tell her what was going on. She didn't need to know that my mom or someone associated with her had sent me a letter. Nor was I going to admit that I'd already been poking around in my mom's life, before that note had even arrived.

I jammed my hands into my pockets, and Tracy continued sorting pills. I wished I could bait her to kiss me again, to rub and touch me and let me put my hands where they didn't belong. I needed a diversion, something to take my mind off my troubles.

And take refuge in a woman who was no longer mine.

Three

Tracy

As soon as I woke up, the first thing that entered my mind was Dash. As much as I dreaded seeing him this morning, I was oddly aroused, too, just knowing that he was nearby.

Damn, but I hated feeling this way. I even rubbed my arms, trying to shed the tingly sensation.

I sat up and squinted at the light peeking through the blinds. This was the only room in the house that I hadn't redecorated. The girlish decor remained the same as when I used to live here. I'd removed the celebrity posters, though. The photos of the country stars I used to admire.

I couldn't begin to guess how many posters of Dash were out there, gracing people's walls. Maybe I should creep into the living room and take a picture of him crashed out on the sofa and make a poster out of it.

Wouldn't that give his loyal Dashers a thrill?

I cleared my cynical thoughts and climbed out of bed. I was fairly certain that Dash wasn't awake yet. He'd never really been a rise-and-shine guy. I'd always gotten up before him.

I headed to the bathroom, washed my face, brushed my teeth and put my hair in a ponytail. I would shower later, just in case Dash stumbled down the hall, needing to pee. I didn't want him banging at the door.

I finished quickly and rounded the corner, poking my head into the living room. I was wrong. Dash wasn't asleep. He was already up and about. I spotted him in the kitchen.

I strolled in there, even if I wanted to go back to bed and hide under the covers. He glanced up at me, and the tingling sensations came rushing back.

"Hi," he said, checking me out with a half smile, as if seeing me in my pajamas pleased him.

At least my ensemble was modest. He wasn't wearing a shirt, and I could've kicked him for it. He wasn't leaving much to the imagination, with that broad chest, those trained-to-perfection abs, the line of hair just below his navel that disappeared into his sweatpants.

"What are you concocting?" I asked, eyeing the mixing bowl and other things lined up on the counter.

"I'm going to make pancakes for your dad. For you, too, if you want some."

"Since when did pancakes become your specialty?" He'd never been much of a cook when we were together.

"Since right now." His smile turned a bit more crooked. "When I checked on your pop earlier, I asked him what he wanted for breakfast, and he said flapjacks." He lifted his phone off the counter. "I googled how to make them from scratch, and this is as far as I got."

He was watching a recipe video? I almost smiled, too. But I was trying not to be too friendly. Or too dreamy. I didn't want him affecting me the way he was. "How long have you been up?"

"About an hour. I wanted to get a jump on everything and prove my worth around here." He set down his phone next to a carton of eggs. "I fed the horses and checked on the foals. There's some cute babies out there."

I sucked in my breath. I didn't want to hear him talk about babies, not even the equine kind. But it wasn't just the child we'd lost that made me hurt. I had some current fertility issues that I hadn't told anyone about. "You went outside dressed like that?"

Dash glanced down at himself. "I've got my boots on."

Yes, he was wearing a pair of rugged black cowboy boots, with his sweatpants tucked into them. "What about a shirt?"

"The horses don't care what I'm wearing. Besides, I'm going to hop in the shower after breakfast, and I'll put a shirt on then."

I sighed. "I haven't showered yet, either."

He waggled his eyebrows. "Well, aren't we the dirty ones?"

I ignored his double entendre. But disregarding him wasn't so easy. He looked deliciously messy, his hair falling in uncombed disarray, his jaw peppered with beard stubble.

I hastily said, "I'm going to check on Pop and see if he needs anything. If you want help with breakfast, I can do that as soon as I come back."

Dash removed a whisk from the utensil caddy. "Thanks. But I can handle it."

I left him to his task and made my way to Pop's room.

Since his door was partially open, I peeked in and got his attention. "Can I come in?"

"Sure," he replied, waving me forward.

I approached the side of his bed. He was propped against the headboard, using several pillows behind his back. I thought he looked tired, but I was glad that he was resting, like he was supposed to. I wanted nothing more than for him to get well.

"How are you feeling?" I asked.

"Still a little swollen, but other than that, I'm okay."

"Do you need an ice pack?"

"I'm using one as we speak." He gestured to his blanket-draped lap. "Dash got it for me."

"He's certainly been busy this morning." Tomorrow I would get up earlier than I did today, hopefully beating him to the punch. "He's trying to figure out how to make the pancakes."

"Really? He didn't tell me he didn't know how to make them."

"He's using a video as his guide."

Pop chuckled. "He's a good kid."

Dash had never seemed like a kid to me. But I wasn't an old cowboy like my dad. I was the lovestruck girl who should've been Dash's wife. "I offered to help him in the kitchen, but he said that he could handle it."

My father studied me for a silent second. "How's it going otherwise?" he asked. "Are you two getting reacquainted?"

Yes? No? Sort of? "We're doing fine. But I'm still not making a record with him."

"I wasn't going to pester you about that." Pop grinned, his tired blue eyes twinkling. "Not today, anyhow."

"But you'll do it on another day, huh?"

"Probably." He laughed, then winced. "Ooh, I felt that."

I reacted with immediate concern. "I can get you a pain pill. You're going to need your antibiotics, too. But it might be better to take them with food, so you don't get queasy."

"I can wait until breakfast."

I tried for a smile. "I'll go make sure it's edible."

He returned my smile. "Thanks, sweetie. I love you."

"I love you, too." I'd gotten lucky having him as my daddy.

I made my way back to the kitchen, and everything seemed hunky-dory. No scorched skillet or lumpy pancakes.

I stood back and watched. Dash was in the process of flipping the next one and looked damned fine doing it. He even had a sexy dusting of flour on his sweatpants.

He shot me a sideways glance, and I wet my lips. I could've eaten him alive, devouring his mouth with mine. Lucky for me, I'd vowed never to kiss him again.

"Are you hungry?" he asked.

Was he kidding? He was making me famished, only with the wrong kind of appetite. "I could eat a small stack, I guess. But I'm going to get Pop his, first."

"Sure. Okay." He completed another perfect pancake.

I fixed my father a plate, along with a glass of orange juice and a cup of black coffee. I also removed his meds from the pillbox I'd prepared yesterday. He was supposed to take the antibiotics three times a day.

I put everything on a tray and brought it to him.

Pop was impressed that my ex had nailed the pancakes on his first try.

When I returned to the kitchen, I noticed that Dash had put on a T-shirt.

"You got dressed," I said, stating the obvious. "I thought you weren't going to do that until after your shower."

"I didn't want to offend you while we were eating."

Offending me wasn't the problem. But I was glad that he'd covered up. I didn't need to drool over him any more than I already had.

I set the table, and he poured us both some coffee.

"Do you still take mounds of that French vanilla creamer in yours?" he asked.

I nodded and went to the fridge to get it. "Do you still like yours with just a bit of sugar and splash of milk?"

"Yes, ma'am." He waited for me to sit before he took his seat.

He was behaving like a proper Southern boy, I thought. Or as proper as a guy from the wrong side of the tracks could be.

"You look cute in your pj's," he said.

My pajamas weren't anything special, just plain blue cotton with a simple green trim. "You don't have to pay me compliments."

"I wasn't just saying it. I mean it. I always liked that you could be natural or glamorous. I could never decide which side of you was more appealing."

"There's no difference. I'm the same person, either way."

"Yeah, but it makes you seem different, like twins or something."

I foolishly asked, "Have you ever dated twins?" I shouldn't care who he played around with, but it was too late to take the question back.

"No. That would be weird, I think. I'd rather have one woman who seems like two."

Meaning what? That he would rather have me? Or someone who reminded him of me? I'd tried to replace him in bed. But none of my other lovers had ever satisfied me the way he did.

I reached for the syrup and poured it over my pancakes. I set down the bottle, and Dash picked it up and doused his, too. I noticed how slowly it dripped.

Thick and sweet and sticky…

I cut into mine and took a bite. How was I going to survive two whole weeks of this? Or however long it turned out to be?

I looked up and saw that he was staring at me. I had syrup on my lips, but now I was too self-conscious to lick it off.

Finally, he sipped his coffee, and I used my napkin to wipe my mouth.

"I'll do the dishes when we're done," I said, interrupting the silence. "I'll clean the kitchen, too."

He glanced toward the stove. He'd spilled batter all over it. "I'm not leaving that mess for you."

"You aren't the tidiest cook, that's for sure."

He shrugged. "Maybe I should've skipped the video and called my chef to talk me through it."

"You have a chef?" He hadn't mentioned it before now.

"Yes, but he doesn't make anything fancy for me. My tastes haven't changed. I still don't like the gourmet stuff."

"Me, neither." Pop had raised me on simple Southern fare, and that remained my preference, too.

"My chef used to work for the people I bought the house from, so I kept him on. I kept some of the ranch hands and caretakers, too. They've been at Pine Tower a long time."

His estate had a name? I should've expected as much. Big, rich places often did, and Pine Tower sounded strong and masculine, just like him. But it didn't matter how glorious his home was. I didn't aim to set foot in it.

We finished eating, and he cleared the plates, intent on cleaning up.

"I'm going to shower now," I said. I figured this would be a good time to get myself together and change out of my pajamas.

He nodded, and I left, still struggling with how anxious being in a domestic setting with him was making me feel.

I gathered my clothes from my room and took them into the bathroom.

As I stood beneath the spray of water, I tried to keep my mind off Dash. But it didn't work. He consumed my thoughts. I even imagined him using the shower after me, standing in the same stall, using the same liquid soap. I couldn't wait until he went back to his regular life. Having him here was killing me, and it was only the first day.

After I was clean and dry, I styled my hair and did my makeup. I didn't make my eyes too smoky, but instead lined them just enough to create a semblance of the glamorous "twin" Dash had accused me of being.

I dragged on a pair of skinny jeans and tied my blouse in front. Then I returned to my room and pulled on my boots, checking my reflection in the full-length mirror.

With a steadying breath, I went to find Dash to tell him the bathroom was free.

By now the kitchen was clean, and he was in the living room, studying a grouping of framed photos on the fireplace mantel. I moved closer, and he turned toward me.

He said, "I was just looking at your mom's pictures and thinking about how much you favor her."

"You used to say that before."

"I know. But it's been a while since I've seen these pictures, and you look even more like her now."

That was true. I did. As for Dash, he favored his father. But I'd never seen a picture of his mother, so I didn't really know what she looked like. Soon after she'd left, his dad had destroyed all of her photos. He'd kept the ones that Dash was in, but he'd scribbled over his ex-wife's face with a marker. He was sorry for his actions later, though, and cried about it, wishing that she would come back to him. Even after she'd betrayed him, he'd claimed that he'd never stopped loving her.

Dash, on the other hand, had rejected the idea of ever falling in love. He'd made up his mind, at twelve years old, that he would never let it happen to him.

I'd been fascinated with love since I'd walked my bridal Barbie down the aisle. But my parents had set a beautiful example. I'd grown up in a house brimming with love.

I'd lost my sweet mama without ever getting to say goodbye. On a Monday evening in late September, she'd died in a car crash on her way home from work. Sometimes Mondays still made me sad. The month of September, too. Just the leaves changing colors could trigger grief. But mostly I celebrated my mother's life. I'd learned to do that from Pop.

"This is my favorite," I said, pointing to a photograph of my parents together, a candid shot taken about a year before she was gone.

Dash traced the edge of the frame. "They look happy."

"They were." So very happy.

He paused, then lowered his hand. "Do you still have any pictures of us together?"

I hesitated, too, and shifted my gaze to his. "Yes, I still have them. They're in an old digital file." The most difficult ones were from when I was pregnant.

I'd never really gotten a noticeable baby bump, but our child had still been there, growing inside me. I dared to ask, "Did you keep any of them?"

He nodded. "We look so young in them."

"We were young." But I didn't want to think about who we used to be. Or who we were now. I was already suffering from seeing him again.

He reached out as if he meant to touch me, but I stepped back, making sure that he didn't.

"You should go take your shower," I said, needing to be rid of him.

He frowned. "Yeah, I guess I should."

He walked away, but it didn't help. I was still affected by him—in my mind, in my body.

But mostly in my heart.

Two days later, I put a plan in motion. I needed to shatter my feelings for Dash. I needed to purge my fertility issues, too. I decided it was time to talk to Alice, my closest and dearest friend, about the secret I'd been keeping.

I called and asked if she was free this afternoon, and she invited me to her house for lunch. Now all I had to do was check in with Dash.

I went outside. It was a lovely summer day, and he was sitting on the patio, taking in the air. He'd spent time with Pop's prize stud this morning, working him in the round pen. Dash had always been a natural horseman.

He glanced up at me, then shielded his eyes from the sun.

I inched closer. "Can I ask you a favor?"

"Sure." He moved his chair to avoid the glare. "What is it?"

"I'm having lunch with a friend, and I wondered if you'd keep an eye on Pop while I'm gone." My father was sleeping for now, and I didn't want to disturb him.

"Of course, I can. That's what I'm here for."

"Thank you." A moment later, I said, "Actually, you have a business association with my friend's husband. Alice is married to Spencer Riggs." Spencer was a renowned songwriter that Dash was supposed to work with on his next album. Funny how people could be connected that way. But it only stood to reason that the hottest new songwriter and the hottest new country star would be planning on making hits together. "I've known Alice for a long time."

"Is she the one who helped jumpstart your career?"

"Yes." My debut album was a compilation of songs written by her late mother, and Alice had been involved in hiring me to record them.

"I heard that Spencer got married while I was on tour, but I didn't pay much attention to it. I don't know him that well yet. I've only met him a few times, but as soon as I'm ready to go back to work, I'm going to call him."

"He's a good guy. I think you'll enjoy collaborating with him. I was in their wedding party. I performed at the reception, too." It had been a beautiful experience, seeing Alice and Spencer so happy.

"Maybe we can get together with them sometime."

I blinked. "What?"

"To go to dinner or something."

"The four of us?" I shook my head, taking a moment to catch my breath.

He pulled a hand through his hair. "It might be a nice way for you and me to become friends again."

By hanging out with a married couple? I couldn't fathom it. "I think we should keep our relationships with them separate. We shouldn't fuss about trying to become friends, either." I didn't want to do anything with Dash, except get these next couple of weeks over with and hopefully never see him again.

He dusted dirt from his jeans, brushing his hands over his knees. "It was just an idea."

He sounded disappointed. But I couldn't cater to his whims. I'd done that when we were together, giving in to whatever he wanted, even if it hurt me. The first time I'd told him that I loved him, he'd freaked out and asked me to never say it again. Of course, I'd thought that I could cure him. That, eventually, he would accept being loved and would fall desperately in love with me, too.

I hurried up and said, "When Pop wakes up from his nap, he's probably going to want to go for his walk." He'd been getting a little exercise each day like he was supposed to.

"That's not a problem. I can go with him. We can stroll down to the barn and back."

Dash was definitely making my father's recovery easier. But that didn't mean I had to be friends with him. "I know that Pop appreciates your help. You've been wonderful with him."

"I'm glad to do it. I'd be glad to help you in any way I can, too. I want to make a difference in your life, Tracy."

I gripped the back of an empty chair. Did he have to be so accommodating? So willing? So irresistible? "I won't be gone long. Maybe a few hours or so."

"Okay." He spoke softly. "See you then."

I turned to leave. But unfortunately, I could feel Dash watching me. He was always roaming his gaze over every inch of my body, making me feel warm and dizzy and forbidden.

A short time later, I arrived at Alice's house, and she greeted me at the door. She lived in a beautifully renovated home that Spencer had purchased when he was still a bachelor. In addition to his songwriting, he ran a dog rescue on the property, which was where he was this afternoon.

I went inside, and Alice reached out for our customary hug. She was a stunning blonde with short, spiky hair, and always wore the latest clothes. Although her primary ties were to the Nashville music scene, she worked as a fashion stylist.

After she prepared lunch, we took it outside and sat beside the pool, with its sparkling blue water.

We dined on salad, turkey-and-cheese sandwiches and a pitcher of sweet tea. For dessert, she provided an assortment of cookies her pastry-chef sister had made.

"I'm so glad your dad is doing well," she said. "I have a box of cookies to send home with you for him."

"Thank you." I'd told her over the phone that Dash was helping with Pop's care. She knew my entire history with Dash. Alice and I had been confiding in each other since we'd first met.

"I can't imagine what it's like for you to have to see Dash every day," she said.

"It's driving me batty." I attacked my salad, stabbing a cherry tomato. "You know how I was already struggling with his fame, and now I wake up every morning and there he is. I think about him when I shouldn't be, like when I'm in bed or in the shower."

Alice stirred her tea, making the ice in her glass swirl. "I know what that's like. I used to do that when I was trying to manage my feelings for Spencer."

And now they were married and planning a family. But it was different for me. I wasn't getting back together with Dash. But nonetheless, I needed to say what I'd come here to say. I braced myself and started with, "There's something important I need to tell you. Something I should have told you before now."

She leaned forward. "About what?"

I winced. "The likelihood that I'll never have kids." I went on to explain, as thoroughly as I could. "I started having irregular periods a while ago, but I thought it was stress, so I didn't see a doctor right away. I knew I wasn't pregnant because I hadn't slept with anyone in the last six months." I gathered my thoughts, troubled as they were. "My ob-gyn ran some tests and discovered what was wrong. I've got something called premature ovarian failure. It means that my ovaries aren't releasing eggs regularly and aren't generating normal estrogen levels."

"Oh, Trace. I'm so sorry. I didn't know that was possible for someone so young. You're not even thirty yet."

"It can happen to women and girls even younger than me."

Alice looked worried. "It's not life-threatening, is it? It's not related to ovarian cancer or anything like that?"

"No. But most women with POF are infertile." I felt the tears coming to my eyes. "And being around Dash is making it even harder. I keep thinking about the baby we lost and how I'll probably never have another one."

"That's so sad." She got teary-eyed, too. "Are you going to tell him about what's happening to you?"

"God, no. He's the last person I would ever tell. I'm not going to say anything to my dad, either."

"Are you taking estrogen?"

I nodded. "It's supposed to prevent some of the

complications I might have later, like osteoporosis. People sometimes mix this up with early menopause, but it's not the same thing. The symptoms are similar, though. The doctor even said that it might lessen my sex drive. But that isn't happening. In fact, I'm actually feeling the opposite, getting hot and bothered over Dash."

"Well, that's good," she said, then quickly clarified. "Not that you have the hots for Dash, but that your sex drive is still going strong."

"I kissed him at the hospital when we were waiting for Pop's surgery. I did it to prove how much control I had and that I could kiss him just once and never do it again. But now he's all I think about."

"Remember when you encouraged me to be with Spencer to try to get him out of my system?" She shook her head. "But then I fell in love with him?"

"My problem is that I never really fell *out* of love with Dash." I glanced over at the pool. "I wish there was a remedy for that. Between Dash and my medical issues, I'm a mess."

Alice gave me a sympathetic look. "I know how much you wanted the baby you lost." She picked at her sandwich. "Is there anything that can be done to help you have kids in the future?"

"Some women with my condition are able to conceive on their own, but that's rare. Mostly they suggest in vitro or donor eggs. Only that's not foolproof, either."

"Do they think your miscarriage was associated with this?"

"No, but what if by some off chance, I did get pregnant and then lost it again? What if I'm prone to recurring miscarriages? There's no way to know for sure."

"I don't blame you for being scared, especially after everything you've already been through."

"My doctor suggested a support group. But I don't want to discuss my life with a bunch of strangers. I keep hoping that once Dash goes home, I'll be able to cope a little better."

"I'll always be here. You can talk to me anytime."

"Thank you." Without her, I would be lost.

When it came time for me to leave, she gave me an extra big hug, and I struggled not to cry on her shoulder.

I drove back to Pop's with his cookies on the seat next to me. Once I got there, I pulled into the driveway and stayed in my truck for a few minutes, preparing to see Dash again.

Finally, I opened the front door and spotted him and my dad sitting at the kitchen table, playing Scrabble.

They both glanced up and smiled. Then Pop said, "I was getting bored being in my room all the time."

"It's nice to see you up and about," I replied. Aside from his walks, he'd been holed up in bed.

"Come join us." He coaxed me over to them.

I set the cookies on the counter. Pop was thriving

in Dash's care. It even seemed as if they were family. And they would have been if Dash and I had gotten married and had the baby. But all of that was gone, I reminded myself.

Long, long gone.

Four

Dash

I'd spent a week so far with Tracy and her dad, and it had almost come to feel like home. Today I was alone in the yard, watching the mares and their foals in pasture. A four-month-old filly, with a heart-shaped patch on her forehead, romped past me. She was a playful little thing, leaping and bouncing and crow-hopping, as if she was trying to make me smile.

I was restless, waiting to hear from Zeke. He hadn't gotten word from Customs yet, but he was supposed to receive a report from the lab today.

Would it reveal that the person who'd sent the

letter was my mom, playing a cat and mouse game with me?

She'd always been a master at messing with people's emotions. Even when I was a kid, I knew she was different from my friends' moms. She needed more attention than theirs. Sometimes she even flirted with their fathers or older brothers or whatever guy was around.

My dad used to say that she'd been trouble from the start, but he'd still wanted her from the moment they'd met. She'd been fascinated with him in the beginning, too. She'd swooned over his good looks and noticeable talent. But when he didn't hit the big time, her feelings for him waned. She'd hated being poor. She'd loathed it more than anything.

Mom had grown up in foster care, with aspirations to be rich. Only she hadn't been interested in earning her wealth herself. She'd wanted a man to take care of her, to make her feel special.

If the letter writer was my mother, was that what she was after? To have her son make her feel special, for the kid she'd abandoned to share his success with her? Or was there another motive? I just wished that damned report would come in, with some sort of conclusive evidence.

Suddenly I heard approaching footsteps behind me. They were too light to be Zeke's. He wasn't here with the lab results. I sensed it was Tracy.

As she joined me at the fence, I turned to look at her. Her thick brown hair spilled over her shoulders and down her back. Her blouse was a delicate floral print that reminded me of the wildflowers I used to pick for her from a field near my old apartment. I used to nab flowers for my mom, too, from other people's yards. I'd gotten stung by a bee doing that once, which seemed rather fitting now.

Tracy said, "I just wanted to let you know that we're getting a feed delivery today. They'll probably be here in about twenty minutes, so if you don't want to get recognized, you should probably go back inside soon."

"I will, thanks. How's your work going?" When I'd gotten up this morning, she'd been engrossed in one of her virtual assistant assignments.

"It's fine. I'm just taking a break." She tucked her hair behind her ear. "Pop is watching one of those goofy old Westerns in his room."

"He likes that early stuff. My dad did, too. Except his favorites were the singing cowboys. It doesn't get any goofier than that."

She laughed and nudged my arm. "You're a singing cowboy."

"Not in the movies." I laughed as well, and got a warm, fuzzy feeling from being silly with her.

I liked that she was joking around. But she sobered quickly, as if she'd done something wrong, and we both went quiet. The filly with the heart on its forehead came over to us, and I reached out to pet her nose. Tracy watched me with a sad expression. Was she thinking about the child we'd lost?

"I'm sorry," I said.

She touched the filly, too. "For what?"

"For everything, I guess."

"Everything?"

I hesitated, working up the courage to say what I meant. She watched me, waiting for my response. Finally, I said, "I'm sorry for not being ready for fatherhood when you got pregnant."

She drew her hand back. "It's over. All of that is over."

"I know, but I'm still sorry." As the filly wandered over to her mother, I felt an even bigger sense of loss. "You deserved to have a partner who wasn't so damned scared."

She gripped the fence so hard I feared she might give herself a splinter. I was making her tense, bringing up a subject that pained her. But I couldn't seem to let it go. I'd spent years regretting how our relationship had ended, and now she was right in front of me. I would be a fool to pass up the opportunity to explain how deeply her miscarriage had affected me, too.

I gently said, "I've thought a lot about the baby, wondering if it was a boy or girl. Sometimes when I see kids around the age ours would've been, I try to imagine what he or she would've been like now. Would its eyes be blue, like yours, or dark like mine? Would it be calling your dad a funny name for grandpa?"

Her breath rushed out. "I've thought about things like that, too. But we can't change what happened."

"I know. I just wanted to say my piece." Was this conversation a mistake? Or was it good that I cleared the air? Tracy still seemed sad. I felt heavy inside, too. But that didn't stop me from asking, "Have you ever dated anyone with children?"

"No." She removed her hands from the rail. "Have you?"

I shook my head. "I wouldn't do it unless the kids were going to become a significant part of my life, and I haven't been serious enough about anyone to make that kind of commitment." A second later, I amended my statement by saying, "You're the only woman I've ever been in a relationship with, and look how I botched that up."

She glanced away. I'd made her uncomfortable again. That had become my forte, it seemed.

"You should go back to the house now," she said. "Before the delivery comes."

"Are you coming inside, too?"

She nodded, and we turned and fell into step together. A light breeze stirred the air and Tracy's hair blew away from her face, exposing a pair of tiny silver spur earrings.

"I haven't been to the feedstore since I got famous," I said. "But I should probably stop in sometime and say hello."

"They'd be thrilled, I'm sure. Maddie brags to everyone about how you used to work there."

"I can see her doing that." She was the brassy old lady who owned it, a bleached-and-teased blonde who smoked like a fiend and kept a flask of Johnnie Walker in her office drawer. "Maybe I'll drop by on a day that you're there."

"That's okay. You don't have to involve me."

Damn, I thought. Could she be any more difficult? "I'm just trying to find an excuse to see you when all of this is over."

She stared straight ahead. "That isn't necessary."

I refused to give up so easily. "I want to make it better, Tracy, to at least work toward healing some of those old wounds. I think we should try to be friends."

She tucked her shoulder away from mine, but I still could feel the heat between us. The emotional energy.

"I don't think us being friends will work," she said. "I just don't."

"So we're back to square one?" I countered. No friendship. No future. No nothing. Just two people, mired in a heap of pain from the past.

Hours later, Zeke came by. I got into the passenger side of the car, and he remained behind the wheel. We didn't go anywhere; we stayed in the driveway at Tracy's dad's house. But the SUV gave us a private place to talk.

Zeke looked like his usual self, big and broad and professional, his suit expertly pressed, his tie knotted good and tight. I probably looked nervous; I was fraught with anticipation, eager to hear his news.

"The fingerprint tests were inconclusive," he said. "Too many people handled the letter and the envelope, and they couldn't get any clear prints. They couldn't extract DNA from anything, either."

Well, hell. "They didn't get anything useful?"

"The only thing they were able to do was to determine what brand of lipstick was used. It was from Chanel. Does that mean anything to you?"

"Actually, it does." I released the air in my lungs. "Chanel was my mother's favorite designer. She always wanted my dad to buy her one of their signature handbags, but he couldn't afford anything like that. He used to get her their cosmetics instead. For her birthdays, for Christmas." I glanced over at the report in his hand. "What's the likelihood that someone else, besides my mother, would have kissed that damned envelope with the same kind of lipstick she used?"

"I have some other information about your mother," he said, grabbing my full attention. "I did a little digging and discovered that all of her credit cards were canceled a few weeks ago. They were being provided by her boyfriend, but he took them away."

"They're not together anymore?"

"That's how it looks. She closed her bank account in Mexico, too. My assumption is that she's living on cash now. She didn't have a substantial balance, so it's not going to go far, especially if she's back in the States. But until I hear from my Customs contact, that remains to be seen."

Exhausted from it all, I ran my hands across my face. "She has to be the one who wrote the letter. Now that she and her current lover are on the outs, she's probably after my money. I figured she was, anyway. But this more or less seals it for me."

Zeke nodded. He looked sorry for the way it was turning out. But we both knew Lola the letter writer was trouble, no matter who she was. He said, "I'll text you as soon I get word on her possible whereabouts. Or if I come across anything else."

I glanced at the house. "I should get back inside." I didn't want to pique Tracy's curiosity, sitting in Zeke's car, having a long conversation.

She jumped to conclusions, anyway. When I entered the living room, she peered up from her laptop and asked, "Is there a breach somewhere?"

"A breach?" I parroted inanely.

"Did someone find out that you're here? Or is there a problem with the cameras that your team set up?"

"No. Everything's fine." My problem had nothing to do with her pop's house. "I was just having a routine meeting."

"Are you sure? Because I don't want the press swarming around here."

"Don't worry. That isn't going to happen." After she returned her attention to her laptop, I said, "I'm going to check on the horses." The feed delivery had already come and gone, and I was free to head outside again.

I needed to get some air, but I wanted to see the mares and their foals, too. I was fascinated by the little filly with the heart-shaped marking. I also appreciated how gentle her mother was with her, maybe because I'd never known what it was like to have a loving, caring mom of my own.

A week later, my stint as a caregiver ended. Tracy's dad was doing well and didn't need my help anymore. I didn't want to go. I liked being with Tracy and her pop, but I couldn't find an excuse to extend my stay.

Unfortunately, I still was waiting for more information about my mom, too. Nothing was happening, except for me going home.

I packed my bag, and Tracy's dad walked outside with me to my truck. He looked so much heathier, so much stronger. But his condition would still be monitored.

"Thanks for everything you've done," he said. "I'm going to miss you."

"You can come visit me anytime. Or I can come back and hang out and play Scrabble or whatever you want to do."

"That would be great. Valentine is going to miss you, too."

I smiled. Valentine was his nickname for the foal I'd grown close to. "I was thinking that I'd like to buy her from you." Of course, that was a waiting game, too. She couldn't be sold until she was weaned.

"I'd love for you to have her. We'll work out a deal later."

I wished I could work out a deal to take possession of his daughter. But I couldn't purchase her the way I would be doing with the foal. So far, Tracy hadn't even come out to say goodbye. She'd been in her room all morning. I assumed that she was avoiding me on purpose.

He said, "I guess you didn't have any luck convincing Tracy to record with you."

"No, no luck." Nothing had changed in that regard. "But I'm still open to it."

He nodded, and we talked for a bit more about inconsequential things. He didn't mention Tracy again.

When we said our final goodbye, he reached out to hug me, clapping me on the back in manly fashion.

After he went back inside, my phone signaled a text. I checked the message and saw the "Mom" code from Zeke.

I actually flinched a little. Had he heard from Customs? Or was it some other news that pertained to her? Whatever it was, I was going to find out soon.

I replied, telling him I was on my way home and to meet me there. Then I glanced up and saw Tracy on the porch.

She was here, after all.

She approached me, and we stared at each other. I wanted to pull her into my arms and hold tight. Hell, at this point I even imagined buying her a big-ass diamond and making her my wife, just so I didn't have to rattle around in my mansion by myself. Suddenly my fame didn't feel so great anymore, especially with my mother looming in the background.

"This is it," she said. "You're going home."

Back to Pine Tower, I thought. A big, beautiful, secluded place that I was still getting used to. "Have you made plans for your birthday?" I asked. It was a little over a week away.

"I haven't decided."

"It would be great if you'd spend it with me. We could go out on the town, and you can bring whatever friends you want."

"And get bombarded by the press? I'd never do that."

"Then you can bring everyone to my house. We can have a party there." I wanted to see her again, however I could.

"I don't think I'm going to be in the mood for a party. I'm sorry, Dash. I know you want to be friends, but I can't hang out with you. We've got too much history between us."

"Yeah, but there's fire between us, too." The sexual chemistry we'd been fighting, the heat that made our pulses pound. Even now, it was sizzling, moving through our bodies like a live wire. "You can't deny it's there."

"I don't want to talk about that." Her voice cracked, as though her throat was parched. "It makes no sense."

I disagreed. "I still want to be friends, but I want to get romantic with you again, too." I needed to soothe the ache deep in my body, deep in my bones. "If you give me a chance, we can start over and see where it leads."

She looked confused. "You want us to date?"

I nodded. "We could forget the past. We could let it go."

She searched my gaze. "And replace it with what?"

"Something new and fun. I can buy you pretty things and take you places I could never afford to take you before." I hoped that she understood how important it was for me to spoil her, to treat her like a queen. Even though it shouldn't matter anymore, I was still carrying around the shame of not being able to buy her an engagement ring back in the day. "I understand that you're concerned about the press, but I have access to private restaurants and clubs now." My world had changed, and I longed to bring her into it. "We could even jet off to a private island."

She went silent, and I waited for her to respond, hoping she would consider it.

Finally, she said, "It sounds complicated to me, being with my ex and letting him sweep me off my feet. You never loved me, Dash. So why should I bend to your will now?"

"Because love isn't the issue. I mean, come on, it's obvious that you don't love me anymore. But that's how it should be." I didn't want her pining over me the way she used to.

She stared unblinkingly at my face. Then she said, "No love, no muss, no fuss. Is that your theory?"

"It definitely makes things easier. And that's why I think it'll work now."

She shook her head. "None of it sounds easy to me. I don't need to go to fancy places or let you buy me pretty things. I just need to be my own person." She stepped back, wobbling a little in her boots. "You should go now."

My pride took an immediate beating.

That was it? That was her decision? To send me away? I couldn't stand the thought of us disappearing from each other's lives again, but what choice did I have? I couldn't beg her.

I slipped on my sunglasses, frowning beneath them. After an awkward pause, she walked toward the house.

I wanted to call her back over to me, to grab her, to shake her, to kiss her. But I climbed in my truck, hurt and frustrated that she'd rejected me, and drove off, leaving her behind.

I took the back roads to Pine Tower, thinking about her the entire time. There was a hole in the pit of my stomach. The emptiness of going home alone, I thought.

Once I got there, I stopped to chat with a group of fans gathered at the security gate, letting them stand beside my window and take some selfies with me. Even with as miserable as I was, I managed to smile.

Later, when I arrived at my big sprawling house, I spotted Zeke, sitting on the porch steps and waiting for me.

Instead of heading inside, I sat beside him and gazed out at my property, taking in the cool blue lake, the floating dock, the grassy knolls and thick green forest.

He removed his tie and tucked it into his pants pocket, waiting for me to speak. I turned toward him, and he squinted, probably seeing a reflection of himself in my mirrored lenses.

I asked, "What did you find out?"

He quit squinting and said, "Your mother took a bus across the border, from Tijuana, Mexico, to San Diego, California. She arrived three days before the letter was postmarked. My guess is that she's staying with someone, a friend or acquaintance, and that they picked her up in San Diego and took her to LA."

"I want you to search for her there."

"I will, but what do you want me to do if I find her?"

"I don't know." I couldn't focus that far ahead. "Do you still think I'm going to get another letter?"

He nodded. "Yes, I absolutely do."

"Then I wish she would hurry up and send it."
But in spite of my impatience, it wasn't my mother
who consumed me today. It was Tracy.

And how badly I missed her already.

Five

Tracy

I was back in my own house, sleeping in my own bed. Pop was doing much better and didn't need me to stay with him anymore. But when I was alone like this, all I did was think about Dash.

I was scheduled to work tomorrow at the feedstore, and here I was, tossing and turning. How was I going to get up in the morning refreshed and ready for work?

The feedstore itself seemed like a problem, too, since it was the place where I'd first met Dash. Everything in my life was intertwined with him, somehow.

The most disturbing part, of course, was that I

still loved him. He assumed otherwise, but he was wrong. I was glad, actually, that he couldn't tell how I felt. Nonetheless, it wasn't healthy for me to care about him, and especially not after all this time. But my stupid heart didn't know the difference.

I sat up and tugged at my clothes. I was wearing a pajama tank top and skimpy little panties. It was hot in my room, the summer night humid and sticky. The swamp cooler in my house had gone out a few months ago, and I couldn't afford to fix it.

I had a fan blowing, but it wasn't helping. I turned on the light, rolled up the blinds, opened the window and stared out at the night sky. It was filled with stars.

Real stars, I thought. Not the celebrity kind.

I needed to figure out what to do about Dash. I certainly couldn't lose sleep over him every night.

Maybe my logic was skewed, but my gut instinct was to just have an affair with him and cleanse this crazy hunger from my blood. No dating. No friendship. No romance. Just down-and-dirty sex.

If I controlled the affair, if it happened on my terms, it might give me a sense of power and help me to stop loving him.

Dang, but how freeing would that be?

Besides, I needed a hot, wild romp. Otherwise I might end up feeling like an old maid—me and my failing ovaries.

Should I propose an affair? Should I actually go through with it? Or would it create even more problems? I couldn't be sure, but avoiding him wasn't working. He was still consuming me.

Of course, if I slept with him, I would have to lay some ground rules. And Dash would have to abide by them. I wasn't going to let him take over. I deserved to take a stand, to be a strong and independent woman, without the burden of love.

I reached for my phone and checked the time. It was 3:16. Whatever I did, I had to do it soon, because I couldn't go through this every night. Maybe I would run it by Alice after I got off work tomorrow. At least I could get her opinion.

I turned off the light and went back to bed, hoping that I was on the right track.

And that someday my feelings for Dash would be gone.

The next evening, Alice and I convened in her stylishly decorated living room, each with a Maltese dog on our lap. I ran my fingers through Cookie's fur. She was the one keeping me company. The other one's name was Candy, and they were the first dogs Spencer had ever rescued. Now they were part of his and Alice's family.

"What do you think?" I asked her. I'd just told her about my Dash idea.

She cautiously replied, "I understand that you don't want to have a conventional romance with him. But what if the affair backfires and leaves you longing for more? You could end up regretting it."

"What more am I going to be longing for? I was engaged to him and pregnant with his baby. I can't get those things back."

"I like that you're approaching this as a way to make yourself stronger. And that you'd be presenting him with a set of rules. But do you trust him to follow them?"

"He won't have a choice if he wants me back in his bed."

She angled her head, her platinum hair illuminated by a multicolored chandelier. "It sounds like he wants more than that, though."

"Because he wants to take me out and buy me nice things?" I shifted in my seat. "How is that relevant?"

"What about his apology about the past? About not being ready for fatherhood when you got pregnant?"

"That doesn't change anything. Nor does it make him capable of love. He was clear about his stand on that."

She sighed. "It's not good that you still love him."

In the silence that followed, I petted Cookie again, and the dog snuggled deeper into my lap. Alice fussed over Candy, too, straightening her glittery pink bow. The dogs were orphaned sisters that had lost their original owner when she'd died. Spencer had found them, alone and afraid, hiding under his porch.

I glanced up and said, "You know the saying 'absence makes the heart grow fonder'? That's been true in my case. The years Dash and I have been separated have only made me miss him more. But if I fight it head-on, I might win."

Alice met my gaze. "If you want to have an affair, and he's willing to accept your terms, then go for it. It's got to be better than how things are for you now."

"Definitely." I sat a little straighter, gaining strength from her support. I needed as much girl power as I could get. "But I'm still not going to sing with him." I wasn't interested in a duet. That would give him too much control over me and my career. "It's just going to be sex. Then it'll be over, once and for all."

She smiled. "You look relieved."

"I am." But I was still nervous about following through and making it happen.

Later that night, I debated my options. Should I invite Dash over to discuss what was on my mind? Or should I do it over the phone?

I did neither. I tidied up instead, walking around my house, going from room to room, putting dishes away, dusting furniture, fluffing pillows and smoothing cushions.

Sometimes I cleaned when I was anxious. Other times I made a mess. Tonight, I was in cleaning mode. But it made sense, in a symbolic way, since I was trying to clean up my life.

Finally, I sat down and opened my laptop. Determined to keep things in perspective, I created a checklist, making my rules clear.

Was I traveling down a slippery slope, preparing to sleep with my ex? Maybe. But it was better than obsessing about him day and night.

After I finished the list, I decided to call. It seemed like the safest solution. Somehow, I just couldn't have this conversation face-to-face.

I dialed his number, but he didn't answer. It went to his voice mail. Now I was stuck, sitting here waiting to hear back from him. I considered cleaning some more.

But before I could pick up my dustrag, Dash returned my call. I answered on the fourth ring. I didn't want to seem too eager, which was weird. I was the one who'd contacted him to begin with.

"Is everything okay?" he asked. "Is your dad all right?"

"He's fine." I gazed at the embroidered Home Sweet Home pillow on my sofa. I'd purchased it as a gift for myself when I'd bought this house. "I wanted to talk about us."

"About me taking you out?"

"Yes." I forced myself to say it, as openly and honestly as I could. "I don't want to date or be friends. But I wouldn't mind sleeping with you again."

He went silent on the other end. Like when crickets chirped in a movie to show you how awkward it was. I had no idea what he was feeling.

Was he stunned? Aroused? Offended? Confused?

Or had the call been dropped, so he hadn't even heard my proposal? Wouldn't that just be my luck?

"Dash? Are you still there?"

"Yeah, I'm here. I just..." He hesitated. "Are you asking me to have a one-night stand?"

"I'm asking you to have an affair. I'm not sure for how long, exactly. A few weeks, a few months. It'll depend on how it goes and when we're both ready for it to end." I reached for my laptop and opened the list, doing my best to stay focused, to not get emotional. This was a huge step for me, and I couldn't let myself falter, even if my heart was beating a nervous cadence. "I have some rules that you'll have to agree to."

"Rules?" He sounded wary.

My heart was still pounding. I took a deep breath. "There's only five."

"Then let's hear them."

I went for it, rushing the words out. "First off, you can't sleep with anyone except me while we're together." His groupies were definitely off-limits. "I won't be with anyone, either." Not that I had other men waiting in the wings, but I figured it was only fair for both of us to be monogamous. "Secondly, we're not going out in public or letting the press know that we're seeing each other." I absolutely, positively needed to keep my trysts with him private. "Thirdly, you're not spreading the wealth and buying me things." I wasn't going to be controlled by his money. "The fourth one is that I'm not recording a

duet with you, not before, during or after the affair."
I didn't want him to keep bugging me about that.
"And lastly, we walk away with a clean slate when
it's over. No messy breakup, no emotional turmoil."

"Damn, Tracy. You're really being methodical
about this."

"I just want to keep it focused on the affair." I
wasn't about to admit how anxious I was about getting this right. Or that deep in my bones, I still loved
him.

"But it sounds so…clinical."

I pressed the issue. "Are you interested or should
I just hang up now?"

"Hold on, girl, give me a minute." He released
an audible breath. "Can I impose some rules, too?"

"No," I said quickly. I couldn't let him take over.
I needed to be the lover in charge.

"Can we start it on your birthday?" he asked.

I considered his suggestion. It had to start sometime, so why not on the day I was born? Or reborn,
I thought, and reprograming myself to stop loving
him. "We can get together that day, but you have to
promise to abide by my rules."

"I will, but can we at least try to make it seem
like a date?"

I challenged him. "It won't change anything. It'll
still just be sex."

"Yeah, but it'll make me feel better for us to treat
it like a date." His voice turned raspy. "I want to
be with you, Tracy. On your birthday, with you hot

and naked in my bed. But I want to wine and dine you, too."

I fought a shiver. He was making me feel warm and sensual. But I still needed to hang tough. "You can wine and dine me at your house. But not anywhere else." I wasn't going to let him con me into going out in public with him. I wasn't going to date him for real.

"Okay," he conceded. "You can come over, and I'll have my chef prepare a meal. We can crack open a bottle of wine and soak in the hot tub, too. Will you stay the night? I'd really like it if you would."

Should I sleep at his house?

"Yes," I said. "I'll stay." It seemed less emotional than coming home late at night, disheveled, with the scent of his skin on mine. At least I could shower and change my clothes at his place in the morning. "I'll pack what I need."

"I'll have Zeke come get you."

"I can take my truck."

"If you're trying to keep this under wraps, then it would be better if your truck isn't spotted driving through my security gate. I've got some diehard Dashers who sometimes hang out there, and they might snap a picture of you or the license plate on your truck."

"Okay, I'll ride with Zeke." I definitely didn't want Dash's fans figuring out who I was and plastering my information all over the internet.

"I'm looking forward to seeing you."

"Me, too." I was also looking forward to shaking him from my blood, to living the rest of my life without my heart being entangled with his.

This affair had better cure me of my ills. If it didn't, I would just be sleeping with the man I reluctantly loved, with no relief in sight.

I fussed over what to wear on my birthday. I finally decided on a skintight dress and tall, sexy boots, making myself look like a sultry cowgirl. For the final touch, I curled my hair, tumbling it into massive waves.

Zeke picked me up, wearing his customary suit and driving the same luxury SUV I'd seen him in before.

I rode in the back seat, and I could feel him glancing at me from time to time in the rearview mirror. We didn't speak during the drive, other than for him to ask me if I wanted him to turn on the radio.

I agreed, and we listened to a country station. When one of Dash's hits came on, I wished I'd opted to leave the radio off. Hearing his twangy voice only made me more nervous.

As we traveled farther into the country, I gazed out the window. Plants and trees bloomed along the way, making everything look soft and summery.

We arrived at the gate, and sure enough, there were fans hanging around. Thank goodness they couldn't see me in the back seat, not through the darkly tinted windows.

Once we drove onto the property, and Dash's house came into view, I sat a little more upright. Now I understood why it was called Pine Tower. The blue-and-white country-style mansion was surrounded by a forest. There was also a private lake with ducks floating on the water. I assumed the equestrian facility was beyond the house somewhere.

"How many acres is this?" I asked Zeke. The sun was beginning to set, creating a hush over the land.

"Altogether, it's about three hundred." He gestured to his left. "I live in one of the guesthouses across the lake. So do Chef and some of the other staff."

"It's really impressive." Dash had gotten everything he'd always wanted.

And now he was going to have me, too. For a little while, anyway.

I glanced up and saw that he'd just come outside and was waiting for us on the wraparound porch. He looked like a mirage. The man I used to know. The man who'd become a star.

Zeke parked the SUV and opened my door for me. As he went around the back to remove my overnight bag, Dash started down the porch steps. When he smiled, I got warm all over.

I returned his smile, determined to enjoy the moment. And when he kissed me, I damned near melted. I slid my arms around his waist, relishing the feel of his whip-hard body against mine. I tucked my hands into the back pockets of his jeans, getting a nice tight grip on his butt, and we both sucked in our breaths.

Zeke cleared his throat, and we separated. By then, my bag had already been moved onto the porch.

After the bodyguard bade us goodbye and drove off, Dash kissed me again, and I rubbed against him. We hadn't even gone into the house yet, and we were already getting intimate.

Finally, he whispered, "Happy Birthday," in my ear.

Happy, indeed. I was tingling, my nipples hard beneath my low-cut bra, my panties silky against my skin.

He took my hand. "I'll give you a tour of the house and let you get settled. Then we can have dinner in my bedroom, on the balcony."

"That sounds nice." I was eager for our evening to begin.

The house consisted of eight bedrooms and ten bathrooms. The main floor featured built-in bookcases, wood-burning fireplaces, a cozy den and a sunny kitchen equipped with an elevator used to serve meals to the master suite. I noticed a breakfast nook with bay windows, too. Also located on the bottom floor were a massive parlor, a formal dining area, a gym and a media room that opened into a music room, where Dash kept his equipment and awards and such.

Most of the bedrooms were upstairs. Dash's master suite offered a glamorous bathroom and two colossal-sized closets.

A staircase led from the balcony outside his room down to a garden with a lap pool and a hot tub.

He said, "There's a patio on the other side of the house with a full-size pool and entertainment area. But I use this one for myself."

"It's incredible, all of it." Every last detail.

"Thank you. You can unpack your bag if you want." He gestured to the closet on the left. "That one is empty. It's for…"

"Your lovers to use?" I tried not to frown. I didn't want to think of other women being here with him.

He nodded, then said, "There's a dressing room inside the closet, so you don't have to come out and change. The couple who lived here before had it designed that way. I can't take credit for how the place was built."

"It certainly seems to fit your needs."

"It's actually bigger than what I need. But I loved the layout. The lake is stocked with bass and catfish, and there's whitetail deer and rabbits and squirrels in the pines. But I don't allow anyone to hunt on the property."

"Zeke told me that he lives across the lake."

"It helps having my top security guy nearby."

"He said that your chef lives in one of the guesthouses, too. When can I meet him?" I'd only gotten a glimpse of him in the kitchen.

"I'll introduce you when he serves our meal."

"What's on the menu?" I'd gotten a whiff of all sorts of yummy aromas when we'd first entered the house.

"Buttermilk fried chicken, sweet potato fries, cheesy grits and collard greens with bacon." He smiled. "A lot of your old favorites."

"It sounds delicious." This was going to be a heck of a birthday. Me and my ex in his mansion, eating comfort food.

"I asked Chef to bake a cake, too."

"I can't wait." I'd always been a dessert kind of gal. The thicker and richer, the better. But mostly I was thinking about being with Dash.

Hot and naked. All night long.

Six

Tracy

The meal was amazing. Dash's chef had outdone himself. He was also a nice, friendly guy. I learned that he lived on the property with his wife and children. I hadn't expected that.

I gazed across the table at Dash, wondering about how many other people lived on the Pine Tower property. Was he surrounded by other families? Did it ever make him think of his own? Or did it remind him of the child we'd lost? My thoughts were shifting in all sorts of directions.

"Is Zeke married?" I asked, as I sank my fork into the dessert on my plate. By now, we were indulging in huge slices of the sinfully delicious chocolate-raspberry cake. "Or does he have any kids?"

Dash shook his head. "He's divorced. No kids."

"Do you know his ex? Or did they split up before he started working for you?" I shouldn't care, but I was sitting here with *my* ex, embarking on an affair. It was tough not to be curious about Dash's bodyguard and if his past influenced Dash in any way.

"It was before. He never says much about it, and I've never really been inclined to ask. His personal life is his business."

I returned to my cake. It didn't matter if Zeke was married or single or if Dash's chef had a zillion kids running around the property. I wasn't supposed to become emotionally invested in this place or its people. Besides, this wasn't the time to think about anything that would remind me of my broken engagement to Dash or the babies I would probably never have.

We both went silent as we continued to eat.

"Do you want to soak in the hot tub after we're done?" he asked a moment later.

I nodded, eager to relax and clear my mind. "Can we bring the wine with us?"

"Yes, but I'm more interested in taking your swimsuit off than playing drinking games." He cut into a sugared rose on his piece of cake and lifted the fork to his mouth.

"I never said anything about drinking games." My pulse pounded between my legs. He looked as if he was letting the flower melt on his tongue. My pulse pounded a little harder. "And just so you know, I'll be wearing a one piece." I watched him take another bite. "You'll have to peel it all the way down." It wasn't going to be as easy to remove as a bikini.

A slow smile spread across his lips. "That's even better."

My skin tingled from my head to my pink polished toes. My bathing suit was pink, too. A deep, dark magenta.

We finished dessert and put our dirty dishes in the bottom of a metal food cart his chef had brought into the room. At some point, Dash's housekeeper would take the cart back to the kitchen and wash the dishes. All he had to do was text her to come by. Like the rest of his loyal staff, she lived in one of the guesthouses across the lake.

Once it was time to get ready for the hot tub, I changed in the walk-in closet/dressing room that Dash provided for his lovers or groupies or whoever he brought home. But for now, I was the woman attracting his attention.

I checked my appearance in the mirror, making sure that my suit wasn't riding up in back. I also pinned my hair into a topknot to keep the ends from getting wet.

I emerged and saw Dash waiting for me. He was wearing beachy printed trunks.

I breathed as deeply as I could. He looked tall and tan and delicious. Clearly, he thought I looked scrumptious, too. His gaze lingered on me, far longer than was necessary, and the reality of what I was doing hit me like a ton of crumbling bricks. Soon I would be naked with the man I was trying not to love. But that was my choice, my way of tackling my feelings. I wasn't about to end this affair before it had even begun.

He grabbed the wine and our glasses, and we took the balcony staircase to his private garden, where the hot tub awaited.

"I might take a quick lap in the pool first," he said, as we reached the bottom. "I like to swim before I soak."

"That's fine." I glanced around. The patio was beautiful, with all the plants and flowers and the artfully strung lights.

Dash turned on the jets. "You're all set."

"Thank you." I poured myself some wine and settled into the hot tub while he dived into the pool. He was a strong swimmer, and watching him made me hungry to touch him. But seeing him in this environment also made him seem larger than life. So different from the poor boy I used to know.

He swam two laps, then joined me, taking the seat next to mine. He slicked his hair back from his forehead and reached for the wine bottle that I'd left on the caddy attached to the side of the tub.

He filled his glass. "Remember how drunk you got on your twenty-first birthday? I had to tuck you into bed."

"I won't drink that much tonight." I topped off my glass. "Maybe I'll just get a little tipsy."

"To build up the courage to be with me?" He set his wine aside. "I'm not going to hurt you, Tracy."

"I'm not worried about that." He'd already hurt me years ago by not loving me. How much damage could he do now? "I'm drinking because I want to have fun." I wasn't about to admit that I was nervous.

He moved closer. "I've missed you."

I'd missed him, too, so danged much. But that didn't change what had gone wrong between us. "I'm only here for the sex."

"I know." He leaned into me. "It's just an affair."

He kissed me, warm and deep, with the water bubbling around us. Our tongues met and mated, and I wrapped my arms around him. I closed my eyes, as well as my heart. I couldn't let myself feel anything more than physical pleasure.

He ended the kiss, and I opened my eyes and looked into his. We stared at each other, unblinking, unmoving, steeped in the strangely tender moment.

"You need to stand up," he said.

"Why?" I managed to ask.

"Because I want to undress you now."

I climbed onto the bench seat, anxious to feel his hands on my body. "Is this a good spot?"

"It's perfect." He began removing my swimsuit. Down it went, from my shoulders to my feet, leaving me naked, water dripping softly from my skin.

He latched onto my hips, and I breathed in the

night air. I knew exactly what he intended to do, and I welcomed it fully, aroused by the intimacy.

I widened my stance, and he put his face between my legs. I delved my hands into his wet hair, and he kissed me down there. He'd always been good at it. But he was even better now. Or maybe I was just desperate for it.

He deepened the pleasure, and I watched him, thinking how sexy he looked. He watched me, too, glancing up to catch my gaze. We stared at each other again, two people fighting the past. But for now, all that mattered was the way he was making me feel.

Slick. Hot. Wet.

I swayed on my feet, letting him take me to delectable heights. I rocked against his face. My old lover. My new lover. He paused to nuzzle my thigh, and I practically begged him to continue. I wanted more, as much as he would give me.

He resumed his ministrations, swirling his tongue, relentless in his pursuit to make me come.

As soon as the orgasm hit, I gasped out loud, my vision blurring, my muscles quivering. The wine I'd consumed went to my head. Or was it the thrill of the moment? I couldn't stop shaking. If Dash hadn't been keeping me steady, my knees might've buckled.

Once my climax ended, I sank back into the water, and he pulled me tight against him, holding me close.

"Am I going to have to carry you back upstairs?" he asked.

I clung to him. "I can walk. I just need a minute."

He nipped at my earlobe. "Maybe we should just stay here instead of going upstairs right away, and I can give you a repeat performance."

I shivered at the thought. "You'd do it again?"

"Damn right I would." He skimmed a hand down the center of my chest and over my stomach. "I'd do it a hundred times, if you'd let me." He paused for a moment as he stared into my eyes. "Just say yes, and I'll be happy to oblige."

I whispered a breathy "Yes," giving him permission to make it happen all over again.

We went back upstairs to Dash's room, and he removed his trunks and wrapped a towel around his waist. I was already naked beneath my towel, fresh from my second orgasm.

I sat on the edge of the bed and released the top-knot in my hair, shaking it out to its full length. I was nervous again, but only because I wanted him so badly. But he wasn't making a move toward me. He was silent, still.

"Is something wrong?" I asked.

"What? No. It's just that we haven't talked about what to use, and I was wondering if you're on anything or if…"

I lifted my anxious gaze to his. I'd gotten pregnant last time because of a broken condom. But our story didn't end there. Once we'd realized what had happened, I'd gone to the pharmacy the next day for the morning-after pill. As it turned out, the emergency contraceptive hadn't been effective because I'd been taking some herbs that had stopped it from working. At that point I'd begun to believe that our baby was meant to be. But I'd been mistaken. Sadly, painfully mistaken.

"I'm not on anything," I said. Women with my condition could take birth control in case they spontaneously ovulated. But I wasn't going to tell him about my POF or how unlikely conception was. "Do you have condoms?"

"Yes, of course. I'm sorry, Tracy. I didn't mean to make this conversation awkward."

"It's okay. You're just being responsible."

"I'm certainly trying to be." He paused, then said, "Oh, before I forget, I have a gift for you."

I widened my eyes. "You're not supposed to be buying me things. That was one of my rules."

"This is different. It's your birthday."

He went to his closet to get the present. He came back with a medium-sized, shiny black box topped with a big silver bow.

He sat beside me, a little too confidently, and I got a suspicious feeling. "This better not be jewelry disguised in a regular box."

He shrugged, smiled and leaned toward me for a quick kiss. "Open it and see."

I didn't trust him, not one sexy little iota. I lifted the lid, keeping the bow intact. The gift was wrapped in sparkly sheets of tissue paper. It seemed too big to be jewelry, but too light to be something else. I was intrigued.

I removed the tissue and uncovered a gold body chain, decorated with rubies. Jewelry, for sure. An unconventional and erotic piece.

I held it up. Six chains draped in front, one of which would loop around my breasts. As for the rubies, they were everywhere.

"It's your birthstone," he said, pointing out the obvious.

My heart pounded. "It's gorgeous, but you still shouldn't have done it."

"It's too late. I already did. Besides, it's just a little enticement between lovers."

"Then I'll wear it for you." How could I not? I dropped my towel and stood to slip on the chain, hooking it around my neck. "Will you fasten the back?"

He nodded and rose to help me.

When I turned to face him, I caught a glimpse of myself in a nearby mirror. I looked wild and naughty, shiny and pretty.

He trailed his hand along the exposed parts of my skin. One of the rubies on the bottom chain dangled just below my navel. I covered his hand with mine and guided it lower, between my legs. He cupped my mound, and I moaned.

We kissed, and I pressed closer. I undid his towel, making it slip to the floor. I stroked him, and we kissed some more, hot and hungry for each other.

He removed a condom from the nightstand drawer, and I pulled him down onto the bed. He sheathed himself, and I watched him, fascinated by how big and hard he was. I needed him inside me.

I waited for him to slide between my legs, but he said, "I think you should be on top."

To ride him? Like the cowgirl I sometimes was? That sounded sexy to me. "Should I keep this on the entire time?" I asked about the body chain.

He nodded, and I straddled him, eager to make his acquaintance. In the next breathtaking instant, I impaled myself, causing both of us to shiver. I moved up and down, rocking on his lap, creating a slow and sensual rhythm. He thumbed my nipples through the gold loops that encircled my breasts. He toyed with the ruby dangling below my navel, too.

"You look like a princess," he said.

I leaned forward, putting my face next to his. "Is that a fantasy of yours?"

"It is now," he whispered, then took my mouth in a heated kiss.

I met the thrust of his tongue, and things got wilder. He gripped my waist and thrust his hips, encouraging me to buck against him. I took him from shaft to tip, riding him hard and fast. I wanted us to come at the same time. We'd always been compatible in that way, so it wasn't much of a stretch. I knew it was possible. He seemed to know it, too.

Intent on touching me, he played with my hair,

tangling it around his fingers. The chains on my body jangled, rubies winking in the light.

I dug my nails into his shoulders, branding him with sharp little marks, and he groaned his pleasure.

The room began to spin. Or maybe it was the climax building in my loins. Dash was hard and heavy between my legs, and I was wet and slick.

I kept riding him, moving us toward completion. The sound he emitted was feral. He was close. So was I.

A fire burned in my belly, a sheen of perspiration misting my skin. Dash was sticky with sweat, too.

I felt him shudder, just as I shook. We came together, hot and fast and furious.

After it was over, he disposed of the condom, and I removed the chain and set it on the nightstand. He returned to bed and took me in his arms, holding me tight.

This affair was definitely off to a wild start, and I was desperate for every second of it.

We slept naked, and when I awakened the next morning, we were in a spooning position, the front of my body pressed against the back of his, my arm looped around his waist.

Was he still asleep? I could feel the warmth of his skin, the ripple of his stomach muscles. But that wasn't enough for me. I wanted to get sexual.

I kissed his shoulder in a loving way, then asked

myself what I was doing. I didn't need to be sweet and affectionate to arouse him, did I?

No, I thought. I was drifting back to the old days, behaving like the foolish girl I used to be. Old habits and all of that. But it was too late. I sensed that Dash was awake.

He confirmed it by saying, "Morning," in a raspy voice.

I removed my lips from his shoulder and went right for his penis, reaching down to grab it.

"Morning, yourself," I said. He was already half hard.

He moaned and laughed at the same time. "I never could trust you in the daylight."

I stroked him, running my thumb across the tip. "I've always been frisky that way."

"Yeah." He turned around, bringing us face-to-face.

He crawled on top of me, pinning me to the bed. I stared up at him, feeling as if I'd just been kidnapped.

"Maybe we should have breakfast first," I said.

He raised his eyebrows. "And here I thought you wanted me for breakfast."

"I need real food." I was making excuses, though I was trying to keep my head on straight. I didn't like the kidnapped feeling. It gave him too much power, making me afraid that I would never stop loving him.

He kept looking down at me, as if he was trying to figure me out. I couldn't tell what he was thinking, but he didn't let me go.

"What do you want to eat?" he asked.

"Is your chef available?"

"No. It's just us."

"Then I'll have some cereal." Something simple and quick. Anything to get him to release me. His body was heavy against mine. But it felt good, so painfully, dangerously good.

"Hot or cold?" he asked.

I blinked. "What?"

"The cereal."

"Cold." I couldn't handle anything hot right now. He was hot enough. My former fiancé, in his big expensive mansion, holding me hostage.

"I'll go get breakfast," he said.

I just wanted him to hurry up. I was trembling beneath him, my limbs practically turning to mush.

He finally lifted his body from mine, giving me a chance to breathe a little easier.

He climbed out of bed and put on a pair of plaid boxers. Then he turned and said, "I want you to stay naked."

After he'd just gotten dressed? How was that fair? "You can't tell me what to do."

"Oops, sorry." He smiled his crooked smile. "Will you stay naked for me? Pretty please with sugary cereal on top?"

"Smart-ass." I considered throwing my pillow at him. But I was charmed by his playfulness, too. He always seemed to have conflicting effects on me. "I don't like the sugary stuff."

"Oh, that's right. You eat the grown-up cereal."

"Just go get it, and I'll decide what I'm going to wear. Or not wear," I added, impishly.

"All right." He hesitated for a second. "If you want coffee, there's one of those single-serve machines on the bar."

He left, and I decided to skip the coffee. Instead, I poured myself a glass of orange juice from the mini fridge. I debated if I should cover up or remain naked. I split the difference and rummaged through Dash's dresser, borrowing a pair of his boxers, the same plaid style he was wearing. I topped them off with the body chain. It took me several tries to reach back and hook it, but I finally got it done.

Dash returned with breakfast. He saw me and broke into a grin. "Damn. Could you be any hotter?"

"I thought it made an interesting fashion statement."

"For sure." He set down the tray. It contained the cereal, two plastic bowls, two spoons, a pitcher of milk and several cloth napkins.

We ate in bed, as cozy as could be. I sat crossed-legged with my napkin on my lap, and he sat upright against the headboard.

"Do you want to shower with me?" I asked. "Just as soon as we're done?"

He glanced at my scantily clad body. "Is that a trick question?"

"No. But my one condition is that you can't do anything to me while we're in there. Only I can do

things to you." After the way he'd made me feel kidnapped earlier, I needed to get my groove back and
be the one in charge.

He swallowed the cereal in his mouth. "You have
an awful lot of rules."

"Don't worry. You're going to enjoy this one." I
wet my lips, letting him know just how good it was
going to be.

For both of us.

Seven

Dash

Tracy was immediately intrigued by the ceiling-mounted, rainfall-style showerhead equipped with LED lights that changed colors. As she made adjustments, I took a moment to gauge my mood. I wasn't sure how I felt about how things were unfolding between us. I wasn't used to having a lover call the shots, but Tracy seemed determined to have her way. If I didn't behave, I figured she would ditch me and go home, and I wasn't prepared to lose her so soon. I wanted our affair to last as long as possible.

"This is pretty," she said, as the water turned blue.

I was more interested in her, the curvy brunette

driving me mad. She ducked under the spray and crooked her finger for me to join her.

I obeyed, anxious for her to touch me. But she soaped down instead, lathering her luscious body and washing her hair. I stood under the rainfall and watched her. She'd turned into quite the seductress, teasing me, making me wait.

I washed myself under the blue water, too. When it glowed green, Tracy was rinsing her hair. By the time it was purple, I wanted to do wicked things to her. Only I wasn't allowed.

She finally came toward me, and I thought I might die on the damned spot. She pumped liquid soap into her hands and reached out to lather me. I was already clean, but I wasn't going to complain about being extra sudsy.

She started at my chest and worked her way down, rolling her fingers over my abs. I sucked in my breath, and my muscles went taut. My erection was growing, and she hadn't even gotten there yet. She took her sweet time, making me suffer.

Finally, finally…she touched me there, stroking me to full arousal.

Tracy rinsed the soap from my body and dropped to her knees. Now I really was going to die.

She teased me with her tongue, and I put my hands in her shower-soaked hair. Water dripped down my face, but I didn't care. I lowered my head to watch.

She took me in her mouth and rocked back and forth, creating a slow and sleek rhythm. Yeah, I was dying for sure. My fingers were practically tangled in her hair.

She increased the tempo, using her hands and her mouth. I couldn't help it; I thrust my hips forward. She didn't seem to mind. If anything, she welcomed my participation. She even pulled me closer.

I groaned out loud. She looked beautiful as the light shifted from purple back to blue, creating an ocean-like shimmer and making her seem like a mermaid.

She glanced up at me, and our gazes locked. She was sultry. Sinful. The sexiest creature on earth.

She took me deeper, all the way to the back of her throat. Damn, it felt good, with all the ripples of heat coursing through me. I definitely wanted this affair to last. I even got the crazy urge that I'd gotten before, to buy her a diamond and marry her.

But I wasn't thinking straight, not with Tracy down on her knees. Still, I imagined her as my wife, living here with me, sleeping in my bed and sharing my love of music. Sharing my world.

She dug her nails into my ass, and my thoughts scattered. Was the water still blue? Or was it green?

All I knew was that my skin was hot, my blood sizzling through my veins. Tracy was taking me to the edge, as an orgasm continued building in my body.

Engulfed in pleasure, I started to shake and shiver, but she didn't finish me off with her hands. She let me spill into her mouth. I tried to watch it happen, but my vision blurred, leaving me in a fog.

Afterward, when Tracy came to her feet, she turned off the shower and rung out her wet hair. I merely stood there, staring at her.

"You okay?" she asked.

"Yeah." I was more than okay.

She got us some towels, and we dried off in the bathroom. I backed her against the sink, and she looked up at me.

"What are you doing?" she asked.

"I just want to thank you." I lowered my mouth to hers, kissing her, holding her gently in my arms.

She sighed, sweet and dreamy, but it didn't last. She wriggled away and darted off to my bedroom. When had she become so elusive? I didn't answer my own question. I didn't want to rehash all the reasons in my mind.

I followed her, and we both went into our closets to grab our clothes. Neither of us used the dressing rooms. We got dressed in front of each other, like we used to do.

"Will you stay for the rest of the day?" I asked.

"I can't." She buttoned her blouse. "I have work to do, a VA project I need to finish."

I zipped my jeans. "Maybe just for a few more hours? We could take a walk in the woods. Or go fishing or just sit on the dock."

"We can do those things next time I come over."

"And when will that be?" I was anxious to see her

again, but why wouldn't I be, with how challenging it was to keep her in my grasp?

She sat down to put on her boots. "I don't know. We'll have to figure it out."

I persisted, trying to pin her down. "When do you work next at the feedstore?"

"Tuesday. But you better not come there, Dash." She shot me a warning look. "You can visit Maddie on a different day."

Screw that, I thought. I was going to do as I pleased and pop over on Tuesday. Only I pretended otherwise. "Whatever you say." I shot her a half-assed grin. "You're the boss."

"You're darned right I am."

She smiled, too, obviously thinking that I was being compliant. But I couldn't give in to everything she said. I wasn't built that way.

I got curious and asked, "Do people ever recognize you at the feedstore?" It had been a while since she'd had a hit record, but she'd still made a bit of a name for herself.

"Sometimes an old fan will come in and wonder why I'm working there." She finished tugging her boots into place. "People think I should be rich. They don't understand that my success wasn't as big as it seemed. Not like yours," she added.

"I got lucky." But I'd also struck while the iron was hot, landing a number of lucrative endorsement deals. By the end of the year, I would be appearing in vitamin water ads that we'd filmed while I was on tour, racking up millions of extra dollars. "What do you tell your old fans?" I asked.

"About why I'm working at the feedstore?" She stood and smoothed her pants legs over her boots. "I just say that the owner is a friend, and mostly I'm doing it to help her out. Maddie vouches for me and tells people that, too. It's easier than admitting how tough things are for me now."

"It shouldn't be that way." She was just as talented as I was. She should've been a bigger star than she was, especially with her incredible vocal range, and I had the power to put her back in the spotlight if she would let me. But she was too stubborn to consider it.

She finished getting ready, but she didn't do her full makeup and hair routine. She kept it minimal: a long sleek ponytail, a light coat of mascara, beeswax lip balm.

"I need to text Zeke to come get you," I said.

"That's fine. I can wait on the porch for him." She went over to the nightstand, where the body chain was delicately coiled. "I'm not going to take this with me."

I frowned. "Why not?"

"Because this is the only place that I'm ever going to wear it. You can keep it here for me."

"It doesn't really seem like a gift if you don't take it with you." But that was her point, I supposed. Her way of reminding me that she'd restricted me from buying her anything to begin with. "You and your rules." She'd never told me what to do in the past. I cocked an eyebrow at her. "When did you become such a dominatrix?"

Her jaw dropped, her lovely little mouth falling open. "That's not what I am."

I shrugged. I even bit back a laugh. She was properly offended. Next time I should buy her a leather corset and a braided whip and really make her squirm.

I texted Zeke and walked Tracy onto the porch. While we waited for her ride, I reached for her hand and held it, wishing that she had agreed to stay with me for the rest of the day.

It was Tuesday, and Zeke was supposed to drive me to the feedstore. But we needed to deal with my mother first. Another letter had arrived this morning, and he was bringing it to me now.

I was anxious, of course. But I was glad, too, that the wait was over. According to what Zeke had said over the phone, my mom had revealed who she was. She'd even provided a phone number.

After Zeke arrived, we went into the den and stood near a wood-burning stove, reserved for cooler days. He reached into his pocket and handed me the letter.

The envelope had another lipstick mark on it, another kiss, just like the first one. I removed the note and read it:

My dearest Dash,
Did you get my last letter? Did you know that
Lola was me, your mama? I hope so. I really
want to see you. Will you call me? I'm stay-
ing with a friend in LA, but I didn't tell her
that you're my son, so you don't need to worry
about her contacting the press or invading
your privacy. We can keep this between us. I
hope that you can forgive me for hurting you
and your daddy. I love and miss you. Looking
forward to hearing from you.

Sweet dreams,
Lola/Mom

Her number was below her signature. I refolded
the note and returned it to the envelope, then glanced
up and scowled. Zeke watched me with an unobtru-
sive expression, giving me time to voice my thoughts.

Battling the tension in my gut, I said, "I can't
believe she told me that she loves me. That's such
bullshit." The "sweet dreams" line bothered me, too.
She used to say that whenever she got the maternal
urge to tuck me in at night. But this wasn't a dream;
it was a nightmare.

"How do you want to proceed?" Zeke asked.

I debated my options. I didn't want to call. I wasn't
ready to talk to her. But I couldn't ignore her sum-
mons, either, not without the anxiety and guilt eating
me alive. "I want you to verify that it's her."

He cocked his head. "You still have doubts?"

"No, but I don't want to give her the satisfaction of giving in so easily. You can call and arrange a meeting with her in LA. Then you can ask her for a DNA sample. After it's confirmed that's she my mother, you can tell her that I'll be willing to see her." I could've suggested that he take a picture of her and send it to me, but I wanted Mom to know that I meant business, insisting on DNA proof.

"When do you want me to make the call?"

"Later today, after we get back from the feed-store." I still intended to go there this afternoon. I was probably in for a fight with Tracy since she'd warned me to stay away. But I was even more determined to do whatever the hell I wanted, with Tracy and my mom. I wasn't going to let either of them control me. Or define me. Or tie me up in knots.

My life was still my own.

D & M Feed was located on the outskirts of town. The D was for Maddie's husband, Dave, only he'd passed on a long time ago, before Tracy and I ever worked there.

Zeke parked the SUV, and we both exited the car. I'd dressed for the part, donning nice Western duds and a straw Stetson. I expected to get recognized.

Sure enough, I did. As soon as we entered the store, a twenty-something redhead glanced in my direction and said, "Oh, my God." She nudged her husband or boyfriend or whoever he was, and he did a double take. They put their heads together, as if they were deciding if it was okay to approach me.

I shot them a smile, and they came over, telling me how much they loved my music and asking to take selfies with me. I posed with them and gazed across the entryway.

I spotted Tracy at the checkout counter with an annoyed look on her face. Clearly, she'd caught the commotion and realized that I'd disobeyed her.

More customers approached me. A couple asked if I would take a picture with their kid, a little cowgirl around five with soulful brown eyes. Her parents said that she liked to dance to my songs. My heart jumped for a moment, and I thought about the baby Tracy and I had lost.

The girl's name was Jilly, and she smiled shyly at me. I knelt to pose with her, and her mom said, "She's going to remember this forever."

I would, too, I thought, since Tracy was nearby. Jilly got brave and reached for me, so I went ahead and scooped her up for another set of pictures.

So yeah, there I was, holding a child in my arms. I'd done that before with other fans' kids, but this felt different. I was still looking across the store at Tracy.

Soon Maddie rushed out from her office. Skinny as a rail, with her teased-and-bleached hair and dusty old boots, she headed toward me. I finished the photos with Jilly and returned her to her mom.

Boom!

Then there was Maddie, throwing her bony arms

around my neck. "As I live and breathe," she said in her raspy voice.

I hugged her, catching an overwhelming whiff of perfume, hairspray and cigarette smoke. She always smelled that way, sometimes with a nip of whisky thrown in.

"Who's that hunk of beef?" she asked.

I chuckled to myself. She must've caught sight of Zeke, standing like a sentry behind me. "He's my bodyguard."

"I wouldn't mind getting a piece of that."

"I'll just bet." I knew she was kidding. She'd always had a goofy sense of humor, as well as a decent heart. She stepped back, and we exchanged a smile.

The store wasn't overly crowded, but I still spent the next ten minutes taking more selfies with customers. Maddie got in the act and took some of her own, excited about posting them on her social media accounts.

As soon as there was a chance to escape, I asked Maddie if I could retreat to the break room for a while. She agreed, taking my arm and offering to escort me while Zeke stayed on the sales floor. I nodded to Tracy as we passed, but she barely acknowledged me. By now, she looked more sad than mad, making me emotional again, too.

I settled into the break room with its dingy interior and folding tables and chairs, and said to Maddie, "The place looks exactly the same."

"Yeah. But you don't. You're shiny and new." She put her hand on my cheek. "Our boy made good."

If only I'd had a mom like her. Maddie had never had kids, but she should've. "Do you think you could give Tracy a break so she can come back here and say hello?"

"Sure. I'll fill in for her. I can drool over that bodyguard of yours while I'm out there." She paused. "Are you and Tracy friends again?"

"More or less." I couldn't admit that we were having an affair. "I helped her when her dad was sick."

"Oh, that's nice." She stepped back. "I'll go get her." She gestured to an ancient white fridge. "You can have a soda if you want. I still keep them handy for you kids."

She referred to all her employees as her kids. "Thanks. But I'm good." I just wanted to see Tracy.

I waited, eager for her to show up.

When she entered the room, I tried for a smile but fell short. I hurt inside, and so did she. The old memories were reflected in each other's eyes.

"I told you not to come here today," she said, much too softly.

"I know." By now, I just needed to hold her. "But I want to a steal a kiss from you."

"You can't do that." She glanced nervously around. "What if one of my coworkers comes in? It'll give us away."

"How about the utility closet?" We used to go in there and mess around when we both worked here.

I'd even knocked over a whole shelf of cleaning sup-plies during one of our more rambunctious sessions.

She shook her head. "That's even worse."

"You're right." It was toward the back of the build-ing, and someone would probably spot us trying to sneak in there. "Why don't I just block this door with one of the tables? Then if someone tries to come in, we'll just say that the door is stuck. That'll give us some time to put the room back to normal."

She pulled her bottom lip between her teeth, al-ready eating her lipstick off. "Do you really have to kiss me that badly?"

"Yeah, I do." As difficult as this day had been, I couldn't think of a better way to relieve my stress. "Come on, just say the word, and we'll do it."

Was she counting the erratic beats of her heart? Deciding what to do? I counted mine, punchy as they were.

One...two...three...

"I must be crazy to be going along with this," she said.

"Maybe we're both nuts." I hurried and barred the door. As soon as I was done, I backed her against the wall.

She lifted her face to mine, and we kissed. In the passion of the moment, I blocked everything out, ex-cept seducing her. She made naughty little sounds, and I moved against her in a carnal rhythm. I tun-neled my hands through her hair, and she knocked my hat off my head. Apparently, it was in her way.

We stopped to suck in some air, then went right back to it. She kept making lusty noises, and I kept getting harder. I wanted to take this all the way, but I couldn't have sex with her here. But damn, I was tempted. Maybe I should just undo her jeans and work my hand inside, rubbing her in the sweetest of spots.

The doorknob rattled, and we jumped apart. Someone was trying to come in. Voices sounded on the other side.

"It's locked," a woman said, sounding confused.

"I didn't even know it had a lock," came the reply.

"Me, neither. But I think he's in there."

Shoot, I thought. Clearly, they were looking for me. Feedstore employees who wanted to meet Dash Smith.

I put a finger to my lips, warning Tracy to stay quiet. She nodded, and we waited for them to try the door a few more times and give up and go away.

Finally, after we heard their retreating footsteps, I plunked on my hat, and Tracy smoothed her hair.

"Am I flushed?" she asked. "Do I look guilty?"

I nodded, and we both burst out laughing.

"What about me?" I asked. "Am I still…obvious?"

She glanced at my fly. "Yeah, there's still a bulge."

"Like I have a sock stuffed down there? Rock stars used to do that when they went on stage. They called it sock 'n roll."

She scoffed at my ridiculous knowledge. "You're making that up."

"I'm not. I swear. They really did it, and people really called it that. But I don't need to enhance what I have, not when I'm around you." I flashed a macho smile and reached for her, but she ducked out of the way, stopping me from pulling her into my arms and kissing her again.

Spoilsport, I thought.

"I have to go," she said. "This was a longer break than it should've been."

I returned the table to its original spot, as if nothing had been amiss. "You should go by yourself, and I'll follow in a little while. There's probably a lot of fans on the sales floor by now. Word of Dash Smith sightings travels fast."

She didn't reply. She just headed for the door. But she did glance back, giving me one last breathless look.

I watched her leave, struggling with the way she made me feel. The emptiness every time she was gone.

Eight

Dash

The DNA test was a familial match to mine, proving who Lola was. I'd expected as much, but at least that part of the ordeal was done. The rest of it was just beginning, though.

I met with Zeke at my house, working out the details. This time we sat in the front parlor, a room decorated with reclaimed wood and rustic antiques.

"What does she want?" I asked.

"Aside from renewing her relationship with you? She wants to move back to Nashville. But she doesn't have any money to make the move or anywhere to live once she gets here."

"She wants me to relocate her?"

"Yes. She's hoping you'll do it soon because the friend she's staying with in LA is getting impatient for her to go. It was just a temporary arrangement between them."

I met his steady gaze. Zeke's eyes were darker than mine and hooded beneath his brows.

"What was your impression of her?" I asked.

"Your mom? She's a handful, I'll say that much. She cried a lot while I was there."

I wasn't surprised that she'd cried in front of him. My dad used to do anything for her when she cried. I'd been affected by it, too. Those dramatic tears. "Did she tell you that she was raised in foster care?"

"No. She didn't mention her childhood. But it's obvious that it shaped who she is."

Just as mine had shaped me. I got up from my seat and walked over to the window, standing next to the glass, making decisions in my head. Zeke sat patiently, letting me think it through.

Finally, I said, "I want you to arrange to bring my mom to Nashville and rent a place for her to live." What else was I going to do? Leave her to fend for herself and scurry around on the streets? "Make sure it's in a nice neighborhood, but that it's somewhat secluded, too. I'll work out a budget and tell my accountant to release the funds. It'll also include a car, some credit cards and a monthly allowance."

"I'll let her know. By the way, she told me that once she gets back to Nashville, she wants to change her name to Lola, as a way of starting over here. She plans to do it legally, through the county clerk's office. It's a simple process. Basically, it's just a form she'll have to fill out, with a filing fee."

"Lola Smith?"

"No. Lola Dorchester. She thinks her maiden name suits her better than Smith. She's uncomfortable about keeping Smith as her last name because of how badly she treated you and your father."

"It's funny how all these years later, she's concerned about me and my dad." I cautiously asked, "If she was your mom, would you be helping her the way I am?"

Zeke frowned, giving me an indication of what his response was going to be. Normally he was difficult to read, rarely giving his feelings away.

He said, "If I was in your position, I would probably do exactly what you're doing. But I wouldn't be happy about it, either." We both fell silent, until he asked, "Do you need anything else from me? Or is that it for tonight?"

"That's it. I'm going to head over to Tracy's, if she has time to see me. But I can drive myself."

"If you're going to start spending time there, I should have cameras installed around her place."

"I'll talk to her about it." But for now, I just needed to touch her. Quickly, mindlessly, passionately. I hadn't seen her since the stolen kiss at the feedstore. I hope she'd agree to accommodate me.

With the way she was calling the shots, I couldn't be sure.

Once Zeke was gone I called her, and she made it even more exciting. She told me that she had to finish up a job on her computer, but that I could come by *after* she was in bed.

"I'll leave a key for you under the mat," she said.

I got hard just thinking about it. "Will you be naked? Will you be ready for me?"

"Maybe," she replied, all soft and sexy. "I guess you'll just have to wait and see."

Even though she was offering herself to me, she was still being elusive. "What time should I check under the mat?" I practically panted into the phone.

"Late. After midnight. Do I need to text you my address?"

"No." I'd never been to her house, but I knew where she lived. I'd always kept her on my radar, even after we'd split up. And now, after everything was said and done, I still wanted her.

At the stroke of midnight, I got in my truck and prepared to drive to Tracy's, immersed in anticipation.

I took the back roads. Though it wasn't a ranch or farm, Tracy's house was located in a patch of country, near her dad's place.

There weren't any headlights behind me; no one on my tail. I'd gotten lucky that the paparazzi weren't overly interested in me right now. Lots of musicians laid low and rested after a big tour. Unless I did something to spark attention, like getting caught with my ex, they'd be chasing someone else.

I turned onto the road that led to Tracy's house and saw the moon peeking through a copse of trees as I pulled into her graveled driveway and killed the engine. She'd forgotten to leave the porch light on. Or maybe she'd done it purposely. I couldn't be sure.

I used my phone as a flashlight and knelt to lift the welcome mat. I didn't see a key. But I keep looking, and finally in the back left corner, I hit pay dirt.

I unlocked the door and went inside. It was pitch-dark, so I continued using my phone for light. She hadn't made this easy. But somehow, I only found it more thrilling.

More mysterious.

I crept down the hall. I didn't know which bed-room was hers, so I tried the first one, turning the knob slowly and pushing the door open a crack.

I turned off my phone to keep it from shining in her face if she was in there. I crossed the threshold and squinted in the dark. Was Tracy in the bed?

As my eyes adjusted to my surroundings, I caught a sudden glimpse of her. Her back was to me, and she was covered with a sheet. All I saw was the shape of her hair, spilling over her pillow. I couldn't tell if she was naked, but I was eager to find out.

I removed my boots and socks, then stripped off my T-shirt, pulling it over my head. I left my jeans on for now.

I got into bed with her. She appeared to be asleep, but I suspected that she was awake and playing a seductive game with me. I touched her hair, but she didn't stir.

"Tracy." I whispered her name and tugged the sheet from her body, one inch at a time.

She was bare, beautifully, sensuously bare. I traced my fingers down her spine, following the feminine curve of her body. She made a breathy sound and turned to face me. I leaned over her, and we kissed, opened-mouthed and carnal.

Heaven on earth.

I reclined next to her, and she unzipped my jeans and put her hand inside. I groaned and slipped my hand between her legs, giving her the same type of pleasure that she gave me.

We kissed and touched and rubbed. I was hard, and she was soft and wet. It was a damned fine combination. The best.

Together we shoved my jeans down my legs, and I took them all the way off. I wasn't wearing underwear. This was a commando night. But before I discarded my denims, I secured a condom from the pocket. I'd brought several, making sure that I was well prepared.

I put on the protection and braced myself above her. She opened her thighs, and I slid between them, entering her in one fell swoop. I remained still for a second, savoring the feeling of my body locked with hers.

She wrapped her legs around me, and I pushed deeper in and out. But I was careful not to move too fast. For now, I wanted it to last.

I cupped her breasts, and she arched her back, her body feline in its grace. We kissed again, and she roamed her hands over me, lingering over the muscles in my back and shoulders as though they had been sculpted just for her.

It made me feel powerful, rough and strong and male. I could sneak into her room for the rest of my life and still want more. I envisioned her moving into Pine Tower with me. But I'd already had mixed-up thoughts about marrying her, so it was just par for the course.

I increased the tempo, needing to come, to clear my mind and lose myself in the friction.

She clawed my back, urging me on. Clearly, she was eager to come, too. I helped her along, lowering my hand between our bodies and rubbing her where it counted.

A gasp escaped from her throat as her nails sank deeper into my flesh. Would she leave lingering marks? Would I wake up tomorrow with evidence of her passion? I hoped so.

She came first, shuddering beneath me. I lost it seconds later, spilling everything I had into her.

In the silence that followed, I collapsed in her arms and steadied my breathing. She nuzzled my neck. We didn't remain that way for long. I had to deal with the condom.

"There's a trash can by the desk," she said, and turned on a small nightlight.

"Thanks." I removed the condom and tied it off. I stepped over my clothes on the floor and tossed it away. In the light, her room was soft and warm, decorated in pale hues.

"Will you stay until I fall asleep?" she asked.

I turned to study her, our gazes meeting and melding. "Definitely." I returned to bed, searched for the sheet and covered both of us with it. "What about the key? Can I keep it, in case we ever do this again?"

"Yes." She extinguished the light. "It's an extra."

I was glad that more midnight rendezvous were possible. It excited me, making my body hum. But somehow that wasn't enough. I still had the notion to ask her to move in with me. But I remained quiet.

She cuddled in my arms, and I kept my eyes open, like a knight on the queen's watch, protecting what was mine.

She nodded off, drifting into a silent slumber. I buried my face against her hair, then got up to leave.

I didn't turn the light back on for fear of waking her. I searched for my phone in the dark and gathered my clothes. Luckily, I'd put my socks inside my boots or I probably would've never found them.

I got dressed in the living room, as quietly as I could. Would she consider moving in with me? Or would she insist on ending our affair? On letting it go?

I locked her front door and returned to my truck. I couldn't keep obsessing about this. I needed to go home and get some sleep. With my hands firmly planted on the wheel, I drove back to Pine Tower.

Alone, with the moon on my heels.

Zeke took care of my mother's relocation, and in a little over a week, she was back in Nashville. Her new residence sat on a hill, all by itself, surrounded by heavy foliage and iron fences. I was on my way to visit her for the first time now.

I rode in the back seat of the SUV, shielded by its tinted windows. When Zeke pulled into her driveway and hit the remote, closing the electronic gate behind us, I thought about how carelessly she'd abandoned me. How she'd said that she wanted to take me with her, but that her boyfriend—the guy she'd left my dad for—wasn't used to kids and couldn't handle having me around. She'd promised that she would send money and buy me gifts and come back to see me, but she'd never done any of those things.

And now I was paying her way. As twisted as it was, there was a strange satisfaction in knowing how much she needed my money. That the boy she'd left behind had grown into a successful man, beloved by millions. Yet I was still nervous, anxiety buzzing like mosquitoes in my gut.

I said to Zeke, "I'm not going to stay long."

He nodded, and I exited the car. I was sporting a pair of custom-made, hand-stitched boots. I'd paid top dollar for them. Ten grand, to be precise. After what "Lola" had done to me and my dad, I was perfectly fine with flaunting my wealth in her face. It seemed like poetic justice, somehow. But mostly I was still hurting inside, feeling the abandonment all over again.

I knocked on the door and took a deep breath, preparing myself for the moment I would first look into her eyes. Her lying eyes. I just hoped that they weren't edged with tears. She was good at crying, at making people feel bad for her, especially me and my daddy.

The door was flung open, and there she was, the woman who'd birthed me. She was older, but still tall and thin and strikingly attractive. She'd always gotten by on her appearance, using it to her best advantage.

She wore a silky white blouse and slim black pants. Her auburn hair was shorter than it used to be and styled in a sleek bob revealing a pair of glittery earrings. They didn't appear to be designer pieces. They actually reminded me of the costume stuff she used to buy at the Goodwill. Had she sold the pricey jewels she might've collected over the years? Was she being forced to wear cheap baubles again?

"Dash." Her voice quavered. "I'm so glad to see you." She moved forward as if she meant to hug me, but I stepped back, thwarting her effort.

Tears flooded her hazel-brown eyes. Just as I feared, she'd resorted to crying. I noticed her false eyelashes and how voluminous they were. She used to wear them before, too, on the nights Dad took her out. He'd always been so proud of how pretty she was.

"Come in," she said, dabbing at her eyes.

I'd yet to speak. I couldn't seem to find my damned voice. I entered the Tudor-style house. Zeke had already told me that it came elegantly furnished, and he was right. I spotted lots of glass and chrome, offset by carved woods and luxurious fabrics.

"Would you like a drink?" she asked, gaining her composure. "I made a pitcher of lemonade. Or I could fix you a cocktail." She gestured to a fully stocked bar.

"I'll take the lemonade." Those were my first words to my mother after eighteen years.

She swept into the kitchen and returned with a tall crystal glass, garnished with lemon wedges. I took it from her. But suddenly I needed something stronger.

I headed over to the bar and spiked my drink with a double shot of vodka, making my own eff-ing cocktail.

I felt her watching me. I turned and smiled like a snake, toasting her. "To my mother and her lies." I needed to get the venom out of my system, to say what I was feeling.

Her eyes watered again, her bottom lip quiver-ing. "I'm sorry," she said. "What I did to you was despicable."

"Yeah, it was."

She toyed with a gold bangle on her wrist. It ap-peared to be a costume piece, too. I shifted my feet

and noticed her eyeing my exorbitantly expensive
boots.

She said, "Thank you for setting me up here. It's
a beautiful place."

"I told Zeke to pick it out."

She angled her head. "You didn't see it before he
rented it for me?"

"No." I felt a muscle tick in my jaw. "I left it up
to him."

"The yard has a magnificent rose garden. We can
sit in the gazebo, if you'd like. I already turned on
the lanterns out there."

"I'd rather stay inside." I swigged my vodka-
infused lemonade and asked, "What happened with
the guy in Mexico? Why did your relationship with
him end?"

"Hector?" With a dramatic sigh, she plopped
down on a velvet settee and crossed her legs. "He
treated me horribly. He was always ordering me
around, correcting me, making me feel like I wasn't
good enough for him. He comes from a distinguished
family, and they looked down their noses at me, too.
He didn't even let me keep my best clothes or jewelry. He took away the things he'd bought for me,
and I'd already sold most of my other belongings before I met him. I was having a hard time then, too."

Apparently, I'd guessed right. She didn't have anything to show for being a mistress. Unless she was
hiding her valuables, which was doubtful. She'd always been the type who liked to show things off.

"Does Hector know what I do for a living?" I asked.

"No. I didn't even know, not until he kicked me out, and I came back to the States."

"That's when you discovered I was famous? Right before you sent me the first letter?"

She nodded. "It's wild, isn't it? I was down and out and staying with an old friend in LA, wondering how I was going to survive. Then I flipped through the music stations on her TV, and there you were, in one of your videos." She folded her hands on her lap. "I tried to immerse myself in Hector's world. I shut myself off from America and everything that was happening here. And since you're not famous in Mexico, I never came across any news about you."

I took another swig of my drink. "I might make it there someday." I already had songs hitting the pop charts in Australia, Europe and Asia, but she'd probably figured that out by now. Or at least gotten wind of the world tour I'd been on. Knowing her, she'd researched my net worth already.

She brightly said, "As soon as I found out about you, I downloaded your album. I must have listened to it a hundred times by now."

I squinted. "Why didn't you just say who you were when you first wrote to me? Why all the cloak-and-dagger stuff?"

"I wasn't sure if you read your fan mail or if you'd get my letter. But I wanted to get your attention in a way that no one else could, just in case I was able to reach you."

"Zeke had it analyzed. He even had the lab test your lipstick."

"Really?" She seemed impressed by the lengths we'd gone to, trying to unmask her. "I'm so happy to be here with you."

I scoffed at her doe-eyed expression. "Yeah, I'll just bet."

She pouted. "Are you going to hate me forever?" When I shrugged, she touched a hand to her heart. "I'll do anything to make it up to you. In spite of how it seems, I always loved you."

I snapped at her. "Don't do that."

"Do what? Tell you that I love you?"

"Yes. I can't stand it when women say that to me." So far, she and Tracy were the only women who'd ever made that claim, and I didn't have to worry about Tracy saying it anymore.

"But don't your female fans say it all the time?"

"That's different. I'm just an illusion to them. A fantasy, not the real thing."

"Did I ruin you?" she asked, in a fussy-mom tone. "Leaving you all alone?"

"I wasn't alone. Dad was there." I finished my drink and slammed the empty glass on the bar. "And do I look ruined to you? I have everything I always wanted. You should see my mansion," I bragged, intent on impressing her, even if saying it out loud didn't make me feel any better.

She leaned forward. "Are you going to invite me over so I can see it?"

"No. And you better not tell anyone that I'm your son. If you do, I'll cut you off."

"Don't worry. I'm not going to do anything stupid." She gazed observantly at me. "Did Zeke tell you that I plan to change my name?"

"Yes, and I'm fine with it." At this point, I preferred that she become someone new. "I'm going to go now."

She stood. "Thank you for rescuing me."

Right, I thought. Because she was a damsel in distress. The thought almost made me laugh.

But after she rushed over and flung her arms around me, I wasn't anywhere near laughing. When I was a kid, I'd longed for her to come back, to hold me, to love me.

Only I couldn't face it now. I stood stiffly while she hugged me, unable to return her embrace.

She let go of me and asked, "When are you going to come back and visit me again?"

"I don't know." For now, all I could do was take one shaky day at a time. And try not to hurt as much as I used to.

Nine

Tracy

I'd been sleeping with Dash for a little over a month, but my plan wasn't working. I still loved him, aching every time I saw him, every time he touched me. Should I end the affair now and put myself out of my misery?

No, I thought. If I bailed out too soon, that might only make me want him more. My solution was to keep going, hoping and praying that I came to my senses.

Along with my struggles, I noticed how moody Dash had been lately. He could be up one minute and down the next. Nothing was clear, not when it came to his behavior. At least I was consistently frazzled. But I tried to be careful not to let it show. I didn't want Dash analyzing me or my actions.

He seemed happy today, but Pop was here with us at Pine Tower, delivering Valentine, the foal Dash had purchased.

The three of us were gathered in the barn, getting the filly settled into her new home. She already had a people-friendly personality, and she was especially fond of Dash. He adored her, as well. They were a good match.

He would be putting a lot of time into her care and training. He intended to do quite a bit of it himself, but he'd also hired a trainer that my father had recommended.

Pop glanced over at me and smiled. He was happy today, too, just like Dash. But Pop's joy went beyond the horse. He was thrilled that Dash and I were seeing each other again.

We didn't tell him the truth, though. We allowed him to believe that we were a legitimate couple and not just two scattered people submerged in an affair.

"Do you want to go for a walk?" I asked my dad. I needed some time to clear my head, and since Dash was busy with the foal, I didn't think he would care if we slipped away.

Pop agreed to accompany me, and we let Dash know that we would be back in a little while.

My father took my arm, and we strolled along

the lake, the sun bright and high in the sky, the weather warm.

"It sure is beautiful here," he said.

"Yes, it is." The land was green and lush, the water clear and blue. Even the forest seemed enchanted. I imagined fairies and gnomes and other mystical creatures inhabiting it.

As we stopped to watch the ducks, some swimming and others preening, a childhood memory flooded my mind. "Do you remember the report I wrote in third grade called 'How Ducks Stay Dry'?"

He nodded and smiled. "I think I still have it in the file cabinet in the garage, with some of your old report cards and drawings and whatnot. You were such a cute duckling yourself. Your mom and I were always so proud of you." He sweetly added, "I still am."

"Thank you." My heart warmed from his words. But would he still be proud of me if he knew what a mess my life really was?

He turned and gazed at me from beneath the brim of his hat. "Now that you and Dash are together, have you changed your mind about making a record with him?"

"No, I haven't. But you know how I feel about that. How I need to do things on my own." I wished that I could tell Pop the truth about my relationship with Dash. But my plan was beginning to seem odd, even to myself. Who sleeps with someone to try to stop loving them?

Was I going about this all wrong? Should I be encouraging Dash to love me instead? Was he more capable of it than he believed himself to be? Or was I being an idiot, just like I was before, longing for the impossible?

"Are you all right?" Pop asked.

I exhaled a jittery breath. "I'm fine."

"You seem anxious all of a sudden. Was it because I mentioned the duet? I'm sorry for pressuring you about that. If you need to handle your career on your own terms, then it's not my place to tell you otherwise."

At this point, I needed to handle everything on my own terms. But heaven help me, I longed for the kind of love that had bloomed between my parents. Something honest and true, something infinite.

"Are you sure you're okay?" Pop asked again.

"Yes, I'm sure. Let's go back to the barn and see how Dash and Valentine are doing." I didn't want to stay here under my father's scrutiny.

Unfortunately, when we returned to the barn, my emotions went from bad to worse, especially when Dash glanced up from the filly to smile at me. By now, I just wanted to pull him tight against me. To kiss him senseless. To close my eyes and block out those desperate yearnings of love.

Later, when we were alone, I acted on my urges, leading Dash to a vacant stall and devouring his mouth with mine. Judging by his fierce reaction, he was more than willing to be ravished.

When we came up for air, he said, "That outfit of yours has been driving me crazy all day."

I'd dressed for the hot weather in a T-shirt and cut-off shorts. "You've always had a thing for me in Daisy Dukes."

"And midcalf boots." He leaned back, giving me a slow, sexy gander.

I latched onto his belt loops, tugging him toward me again. "You better have a condom on you."

"I always keep one handy now that I'm with you." He dug a packet out of his wallet.

"Just hurry up."

He put his wallet away. "Damn, but you're on fire."

Yes, I was burning up, with passion, with a feeling of do-or-die. But I was the one who was trying to forget about love.

We kissed once more, then dived into a frenzy.

He peeled off my shorts and panties, leaving me in my top and boots. I untucked his casual snap-front shirt and pulled it open in one swift motion, baring his beautifully tanned chest. He shoved his jeans and boxers down, and I watched his erection spring free.

He fumbled with the condom, cursing when he couldn't tear open the wrapper fast enough.

I keened out a moan when he finally thrust into me. He moved like a madman, hard and fast. My bare butt was going to be sore later, with how feverishly I was being jackhammered against the wall.

The stall was clean, but the scent of horses and hay still permeated the air, making us seem animalistic, too, as we panted and pushed and made primal sounds.

I bit down on my bottom lip so hard I nearly drew blood. I didn't even care if someone came into the barn and saw us. But I knew that wasn't likely. Dash had sent his ranch hands away earlier so he could have time alone with Valentine. And now he was getting time alone with me.

Dirty time, I thought. But this was what I wanted, what I needed to liberate my heart. Only it didn't work.

After our orgasms exploded and the sex was over, my problem wasn't solved. I was still consumed with love.

We got dressed and went into the house. And all the while, my thoughts were reeling. Was I being foolish? Or was it possible for Dash to love me? I wanted to believe the best, to cling to some sort of hope. But I was scared, too, of slipping back into my old ways and getting my soul crushed.

"Do you want to listen to some music?" he asked.

"Sure. Okay." I tried to sound more upbeat than I felt, and it seemed as though I'd succeeded. He didn't appear to notice how conflicted I was.

I followed him into the music room, where he

kept his guitars, his studio equipment, his gold records and awards.

While I headed for a black leather recliner, he searched for LPs to play on an old-school stereo he'd built. As much as he appreciated digital music, he'd been collecting vinyl for as long as I'd known him.

In regard to his own songs, most of his lyrics were filled with angst, influenced by his impoverished youth and his struggle to make his way in the world. His chart-topping album had a broodingly handsome image of him on the cover that made women want to save him. Me, included. And I was supposed to know better.

But apparently, I knew nothing. Because here I was, wishing all over again that he loved me.

He glanced up and caught my gaze, and my heart dropped straight to my stomach, where our baby had once nestled. He hadn't written any songs about that and neither had I.

No one except our dads had known that I was pregnant. We hadn't told our friends or coworkers. We'd planned to once I was farther along, but that never happened.

"I still need to call Spencer," he said, pulling me out of the past and back to the present.

"To work on your collaboration?"

"Yes, but then I thought it might be nice to invite him and Alice over first. Or is the four of us getting together still an issue for you?"

"We can hang out with them, if you want." At

this point, I liked the idea of doing a couples thing. Spencer and Alice had overcome tons of obstacles to be together, and I admired them for what they'd accomplished. And maybe, *just maybe*, their happily-married, crazy-in-love vibe might rub off on Dash.

He studied me for a second. "Really, you're okay with it? I expected you to invoke one of your rules."

"Most of my rules have already fallen by the wayside." And by now, I had a new agenda. Mercy me. If he only knew.

"Then let's plan a barbecue, as soon as they're available. Maybe we can all go kayaking that day, too."

"I'll text Alice and see what she says." I suspected that she and Spencer would be happy to join us for food and a paddle around the lake.

Dash continued rifling through his record collection and held up two country blues albums that we'd both been reared on.

I nodded my approval, and he removed them from their sleeves and placed them on the stacking spindle. As the first one dropped onto the turntable and began to play, he came over to me. He crawled onto my chair, sending the recliner back.

I gripped the sides of the leather. "What are you doing?"

"Kissing you." He put his lips on mine, and I swooned like a schoolgirl. He was being warm and gentle, his touch slow and easy, as if he had all the time in the world. And he did, I thought. I would give him the rest of my life if it worked out that way.

My eyelids fluttered open and I gazed at his face, so close to mine. Was he capable of love? Was the shell he'd built around himself breakable?

There was no way I could end this affair without at least trying to find out. But I had to stay strong, too. To keep my wits about me. I couldn't fall apart like before.

"What are you thinking about?" he asked.

A sigh escaped my throat. "You."

"What about me?"

I answered as honestly as I could, without giving myself away. "How amazing you make me feel, about how much I need you."

He kissed me again, and I floated into a romantic abyss, lost in the feeling of him.

The barbecue got off to a wonderful start. I set the table with picnic ware, and the four of us gathered on Dash's patio with his oasis-style pool as the backdrop. We didn't involve his chef. We did everything ourselves, like regular people.

Along with the burgers Dash had grilled, we dined on salads and sides and fresh-cut watermelon. For dessert, I'd made a big frothy bowl of strawberry trifle, and I put that out, too.

Dash nursed a beer while Spencer, a recovering alcoholic, drank ginger ale. Spencer didn't shy away from events where spirits were served. He even kept a bar at his house to accommodate his guests. But he attended meetings regularly, too. He didn't take his recovery lightly, and neither did Alice. He'd nearly relapsed during a difficult time in their relationship.

He and Alice made an attractive couple. Whereas she was blonde and fair, he was tall and dark. They'd both been wild in their youth. In some ways, they'd been cut from the same cloth.

Everyone chatted easily, and it felt good to be in the company of friends. Yet even with as much fun as I was having, I was still worried about what the future held.

Were Dash and I cut from the same cloth? Did we have enough in common to make a relationship work? Or would we crash and burn like we did before?

Every so often Dash would look over at me and smile, but that wasn't helping my cause. He was giving me butterflies. So much so, I'd begun picking at the rest of my food, feeling too fluttery to eat.

After the meal, Dash took Spencer to the barn to meet Valentine, and Alice helped me clean up, carrying the half-eaten salads, sides and trifle inside.

"What's going on?" she asked. "I can tell that something is up with you."

Of course, she could. She knew me better than anyone. "I'm a bit of a mess, actually. I'm still in love with Dash. In fact, I've been resorting to my old ways and hoping that he's going to fall in love with me, too."

She furrowed her brow in obvious concern. "Do you think he's changed, though? Does he seem different to you?"

"He wasn't famous before, so that's changed him. But as far as the rest of it goes, I can't really tell. Sometimes he seems moodier than he used to be. But he's also been really attentive."

"That sounds confusing."

"I know. And if it doesn't progress the way I want it to, I can't let it wreck me like it did last time." I had to be a newer, stronger woman. Or so I kept telling myself.

I removed plastic containers from the cabinet and began scooping leftovers into them. Alice followed my lead and began transferring the potato salad from its bowl to the Tupperware. "You'll be all right. I know you will."

"I'm glad Dash suggested this barbecue. I even hoped that you and Spencer would be a good influence on him."

"Oh, wow. Now I'm feeling the pressure." She bumped my shoulder with hers. "But I'm flattered, too."

I wanted what she had. The love. The happiness. But for now, all I could do was enjoy the rest of the day and quit panicking about things I couldn't control.

After the men returned from the barn, we changed into our swimsuits for our kayaking adventure.

We used tandem kayaks and safety gear that Dash provided from his boathouse. He had everything we needed.

Spencer and Alice climbed into their kayak, Spencer in the rear and Alice up front, and launched off the dock. Both of them were experienced kayakers, so they managed it with ease.

Dash and I followed them into the lake. We had the same seating arrangement, with Dash behind me. Only in our case, our skills weren't equal. Dash was an expert, and I was a novice.

As we paddled through the water, I prayed that I wouldn't lose my stride and rock the boat. But I didn't need to fret. We glided along in perfect harmony, working as a team. Stable as could be, I thought. As if we belonged together for real.

Later that night, Dash and I went to his room to get ready for bed. He'd already stripped down to his underwear, but I hadn't gotten undressed yet.

"I need to talk to you," he said.

"What is it?" He seemed anxious, and I hoped that our relaxed mood from earlier in the day wasn't about to blow up in my face.

He sat on the edge of the bed and dragged a hand through his hair. "Now don't freak out, but I think that we should get engaged again."

I nearly pitched forward. Had I heard him correctly? Had he just proposed? Yes, by God, he had. Yet from the almost distant way he'd said it, I knew immediately that it had nothing to do with love.

I fought the air that had suddenly gotten trapped in my lungs and asked, "Why do you think we should get engaged?"

"Because I enjoy being with you, and I could see us having a good life together."

Desperate to squeeze in the L-word, I quickly said, "Most people think that marriage is supposed to be about love."

"Yeah, but it's different for us. We can still have a close relationship without the whole love thing. I mean, isn't that what we've been doing already? You can't deny that we've become friends again or that the time we spend together isn't fulfilling."

I wanted to cry, but I tempered the urge, forcing my tears back. I'd led him to believe that I didn't love him anymore, and now I was paying the ultimate price.

He proceeded with, "I'm lonely when I'm not with you."

He sounded more emotional now, more romantic, but loneliness wasn't love. Nor was it the bond I was looking for. My heart hurt from what he wasn't saying. The one thing I needed to hear.

He continued to express himself. "Marrying you has been in the back of my mind since we started the affair. But I kept thinking I was crazy for having those thoughts. Then after being around Alice and Spencer today, I realized that it wasn't so crazy at all. That we could be as content as they are."

Apparently, they had influenced him, just not in the way I'd hoped. He'd completely overlooked how in love they were.

"I know our engagement faltered last time," he said. "But that's because I was scared that I didn't have the means to make things work. But I can give you a luxurious life now. You can sell your house and move in with me. I can buy your dad a bigger farm in this area or he can live at Pine Tower, too, depending on what he prefers." He made a grand gesture. "Just think of what an incredible wedding we'll have. I'll get you the dress and diamond of your dreams, and once we're married, you can spend as much time on your career as you want without having to work other jobs. Then, when you're ready, we can record together."

I shook my head. He had it all figured out. Every little detail of how he was going to manipulate my life. "Are you even listening to yourself, Dash? You're making this all about your success, and how grateful I'm supposed to be for it."

"Oh yeah?" he shot back. "Well, some support from you would be nice, some pride in how far I've come. You know damn well that I grew up with nothing, and it made me feel like nothing."

"Yes, but that doesn't give you the right to try to buy me off now."

A muscle pulsed at his neck. "There's nothing wrong with a man wanting to take care of his wife."

I defended my position. "And there's nothing wrong with a woman who prefers to take care of herself."

He stood and came over to me. "Can't you at least consider marrying me?"

"Not like this." I couldn't tell him the real reason I was turning him down. Or how painful it was to be this close to him, longing for more.

"Are you going to stop seeing me?" he asked. "Is this the end of our affair?"

I hesitated to answer, not knowing what to do.

"Tracy?" he persisted.

I wasn't ready to let him go. I should be, but I couldn't seem to walk away. People in love acted foolishly, and I was no exception. "We can keep it going for a while. Unless you want to end it."

"I'm not going to be the one to call it quits. Not after I just offered to share my damned life with you."

Okay, then. We were staying together for now, as awkward as you please, emotions still raw between us.

He went over to the bed and turned down the sheet. "It's getting late. We should get some sleep."

I began removing my clothes, but not all of them.

Since he was in his boxers, I left my underwear on, too: a tan bra and low-rise panties. We climbed under the covers, but we didn't touch.

He turned off the light, and I closed my eyes, lying fitfully next to him, tangled up in an affair that had gone horribly awry.

Ten

Dash

I spent the week after Tracy turned down my proposal shopping online, stewing in my own frustration and buying gifts for my mom.

At first, I didn't know if I was willing to see her again, and now I was making outrageous purchases. But at least Mom would appreciate whatever I gave her. I was only doing this to combat Tracy's rejection, but I needed to feel useful.

I was hurt and angry at the way Tracy had reacted to my proposal. Granted, I'd just sort of thrown it out there, but I was trying to share my home with her, to make music together, to be lifelong partners.

I'd assumed that comparing us to Alice and Spencer would've worked in my favor. But clearly, it hadn't.

Why did Tracy have to be so stubborn? Why couldn't she rejoice in my success and give me the satisfaction of showering her with the riches I'd worked so hard to attain? She knew how painful my childhood was and how being poor had destroyed my self-worth. But it wasn't just about me. I'd always longed to share whatever I acquired with Tracy, giving her the things neither of us had when we were growing up. I'd panicked when she'd gotten pregnant because I was afraid of how I was going to give our child the life it deserved. My insecurities had gotten the best of me, damaging my relationship with Tracy, too.

And now…it was a mess all over again.

I glanced over at Zeke. He was helping me load the SUV with the stuff I'd bought for Mom. I hadn't told him that I'd asked Tracy to marry me or that she'd turned me down. I didn't have to explain myself to him. His job was to protect me, not discuss how fractured I was. Every time I thought about Tracy's rejection, I felt broken inside, as if someone had taken me apart and put me back together wrong.

"Is that all of it?" Zeke asked.

I nodded, and he closed the hatch.

Mom was expecting me, but she didn't know that I would be bearing gifts. I wanted to surprise her. In some ways what I was doing seemed twisted and sick. In other ways, it pacified me, especially since I was still hurting over Tracy.

After Zeke and I arrived at Mom's new place, I stayed in the back seat for a minute, gazing out at the night and wondering what my dad would think if he knew that I'd renewed my relationship with Mom. He'd loved her right up to his dying day. But he'd hated her for what she'd done to us, too. She'd had a toxic effect on him. On me, too, but here I was, feeding the fire. Of course there was a lonely part of me that needed my mother, regardless of how twisted it seemed.

I got out of the car, gathered some of the packages and walked to the door. I shuffled the items in my hands and rang the bell. Mom answered it, her eyes going wide.

"What's all this?" she asked, as Zeke approached us, with his arms full, too.

"Just some things I wanted you to have," I said.

"Oh, my." She looked like a cat on Christmas Eve, eager to play with the ornaments on the tree.

We entered the house, and she practically danced around the living room. We piled the first batch on the dining room table and went back for more. Once we brought the rest of it in, bags and boxes overflowed onto the floor. The table wasn't big enough to hold everything.

Zeke backed away, letting me know he would be waiting in the car. As soon as he left, Mom dived right in.

I sat on the sofa and watched her. The first thing she opened was a large black Chanel handbag. She gasped in sheer delight. I'd gotten her the most expensive one in their current collection. She went on to the next gifts, which were two pairs of shoes: Christian Louboutin slides and Manolo Blahnik pumps. She squealed and clapped.

I said, "You can exchange anything you don't want. Or if things don't fit or whatever. I gauged the size based on what you used to wear." Those old thrift store fashions she used to whine about.

She wasn't complaining now.

"This is so amazing." She had tissue paper flying out of her hands. "Oh, look at this." She removed a gold Givenchy gown from its box. She held the garment lovingly against her, twirling, making the fabric spin.

I was rewarding her for hurting me, for tearing me apart when I was kid. Yet her excitement made me feel needed. Why couldn't Tracy need me in this way? The only valuable thing I'd given her was a birthstone body chain that she'd left at my house.

After Mom opened each and every gift, she ran over to me. I stood, and she hugged me. I returned her affection, allowing myself to embrace her, and she cried on my shoulder.

Tears of spoiled joy.

We separated, and she said, "No one has ever given me so many extraordinary things."

I gazed into her makeup-smudged eyes. "Not even any of your old boyfriends?"

"No, not even them. But now I have you, and you matter more than any of them ever could."

Rather than dispute her claim, I grabbed a silk blouse from the pile of new clothes and dried her tears with it.

"Dash!" She scolded me for soiling it. "That's a Versace!"

"Don't worry about it. I'll buy you another one." I didn't care if she blew her nose on it. There were more where that came from. I was only doing this to ease my pain over the woman who refused to marry me.

Tracy visited me the following day. I asked her to come over and hang out, sending Zeke to her house to get her, as we'd been doing all along. But now that she was here with me, we barely seemed like friends—let alone lovers who were supposed to be continuing their affair.

We took a walk in the woods. On this hot and glaring afternoon, the towering pine trees provided some much-needed shade. We could've cooled off inside, but I didn't want to be cooped up right now, not even in a sprawling mansion.

"How have you been?" I asked, trying to break the ice. I hadn't seen her since the weekend she'd rejected my proposal.

"Fine. Just busy with work." She looked wholesome this afternoon, maybe even a bit messy. She had a loose hairdo that was half up and half down, a twisty bun of sorts, with long strands falling around it. Her clothes were simple: a plain beige T-shirt and skinny jeans tucked into natural brown boots. It was the same pair she'd worn with the Daisy Dukes when we'd messed around in the barn. I wished that she was in that kind of mood today. I would let her ravish me in a Tennessee minute, if she was so inclined.

"What have you been doing?" she asked.

"Nothing much." Just buying my mom a bunch of crap, I thought, and trying to survive the ache of Tracy not wanting to be my wife. After we walked a while longer, deeper into the woods, I asked, "Do you want to sit a spell?"

"Okay." She chose a tree and plopped down next to it.

As I joined her in the dirt, I heard a scratching sound. I looked up and caught sight of a squirrel racing up the trunk and heading for the branches. On closer inspection, I realized it was a mama squirrel scurrying around with her young. I tried to count how many there were. Five. Six. I couldn't be sure.

Tracy glanced up and saw them, too. "Oh, how cute. The one on the lower branch is watching us."

I smiled. "It's probably thinking about hiding some seeds in that sexy hair of yours."

She met my gaze. "You think it's sexy like this?"

"Yeah, I do." I thought everything about her was

enticing. The thickness of her hair. The blueness of her eyes.

We stared at each other, and I considered kissing her. But somehow, I couldn't bring myself to do it. I wanted her to initiate the first touch. But she only drew her knees up to her chest, as if she was protecting herself from me.

A moment later, she asked, "Are you going to propose to me again? Is that why we're out here?"

"What? No." Even with as badly as I wanted to marry her, I wasn't going to subject myself to another rejection.

"You don't have a fancy ring in your pocket?"

I shook my head. I even turned my jeans' pockets inside out to show her they were empty.

"I just thought maybe…"

I leaned forward with an inkling of hope. "Would that have worked? Would you have accepted?"

Her breath hitched. "I'm sorry, no. You buying me a ring is the last thing I need."

I shrugged, refusing to let her see how flustered I was. Flustered, annoyed, hurt, offended. If I could get away with it, I would shove the biggest diamond in the world on her finger and make her wear it.

"Do you want to go inside for lunch?" I asked, feigning normalcy. I came to my feet. "We can make sandwiches or something."

She stood and dusted herself off. Was she trying to act casual now, too? "I am getting a little hungry."

Falling into step together, we trekked to the house,

the sun beating down on us, making a trail of sweat creep down the back of my shirt.

We entered the kitchen through a sliding glass door, drank some water and rummaged through the fridge. After a quick debate, we decided on roast beef sandwiches on sourdough rolls with white American cheese. She put pickles and pretzels on our plates, and we entered the dining room.

Before we sat down to eat, I spotted something on the floor, in the corner, next to the weathered-wood buffet. A small jewelry-size box with a glittery bow. One of the gifts I'd gotten for my mom. Except that it must've fallen off the buffet when I'd piled all of the boxes and bags there last night, before Zeke and I had taken them out to the car.

Tracy turned and saw it, too, and my heart nearly stopped.

I went over to where it was and picked it up. I couldn't pretend that she hadn't noticed it.

"What is that?" she asked.

I couldn't think fast enough, so I stalled, panicking about what to say. Did she think it was a ring?

She moved in my direction, closing in on me.

"It's not what it looks like," I said.

She gazed suspiciously at me. "Are you sure?"

"Of course, I am." I couldn't remember what was in that particular box, but I knew it wasn't a ring. I hadn't bought Mom any rings.

"Then what is it?" she asked again.

There was no way I was going to tell her that it

was for my mom. After what my mother had done to me, I didn't think Tracy would understand why I'd let her back into my life or why I was buying her expensive clothes and jewelry. My feelings about my mom were complicated. But they always had been, even when I was a kid. And now that I was an adult, I needed to deal with it on my own. Pulling Tracy into it would only make it harder.

Struggling to keep my cool, I concocted a story. "It's for a friend. It's his anniversary this week, and he asked me to hold on to his wife's gift, so she doesn't scrounge around their place trying to find out what he got her."

She tilted her head. "Why was it on the floor?"

"I put it on the buffet last night, but it must have fallen off." At least that part was true. But I wished that I hadn't been so careless. Even Zeke had missed it.

She squinted at me. "Who is this friend?"

I wasn't about to implicate a real person. But I didn't want to make someone up, either, not at the risk of her checking to see if the guy existed. "Why does it matter who he is?"

"Why are you being so evasive? If you got me an engagement ring, then just tell me. It's not like I didn't suspect that you—"

"Fine. You want proof that it isn't for you? Then I'll open it." I grabbed a butter knife off the table and sliced the tape on the sides. I lifted the lid off the box.

"There, see. Gucci earrings." I recognized them right away. Eighteen-karat gold, jade and diamond drops.

She peered into the box, studying them for a few contemplative seconds. "How do you know they're Gucci?"

Shit. The logo wasn't visible. I knew because I'd bought the damned things, but that didn't jibe with the story I was telling her. "I can tell by the style."

"You certainly have a good eye for women's jewelry."

"Yeah, I guess I do. But I told you it wasn't a ring."

She studied the earrings again. "When is your friend going to pick those up?"

"He isn't. I'm supposed to bring them to their party on Friday night." In actuality, I planned to see my mom that evening. She'd invited me for dinner. "They live in a suburb just south of the city." I added that detail because I was trying to make it seem more believable. The real day. The true location. The designated time. "It starts at seven, but it's not a surprise or anything. It's a cocktail thing they planned together."

"You better tape the sides of the box up again and try to make it look like you didn't open it."

"I'll do that later." I fidgeted with the lid.

She watched me, a bit too closely. "I'm sorry if I put you on the spot about it being a ring. But you're still acting strange."

"It's been a strange day." I set the box down, needing to be rid of it. "Can we just eat now?"

She nodded, and I decided that if I bought Mom anything else, I would have the packages sent directly to her, keeping Tracy from stumbling upon them. I couldn't cope with another mishap.

We took our seats, the silence between us as thick as the lie I'd just told. But there was no way I was going to come clean about who the earrings were for.

My mom was my secret to keep.

Eleven

Tracy

Zeke gave me a ride home from Pine Tower. But as soon as I got in the door, I called Alice, fretting over Dash and his odd behavior. And now I was at Alice's house, in her room, telling her about my concerns.

She worked while we talked, sorting through a box of feather boas for a client and placing them in two distinct piles on the bed. Spencer was out of town on business and wouldn't be back until next week. The two Maltese dogs were nearby, though, curled up in a corner.

Alice frowned. "Are you sure you're not over-reacting?"

I sat on a corner of the bed near the *maybe* pile. "I don't think the earrings belonged to a friend. I think Dash bought them. There was just something about how quickly he knew what brand they were." Something that gnawed at me.

"Then he must have bought them for you. But he changed his mind about giving them to you."

"Why would he buy me a gift like that? They're not anywhere near my style." My heart thudded in my chest. "What if they're for another woman? What if he got hurt and mad that I'd rejected his proposal and went back to one of his groupies?"

"Oh, Trace." She dropped a red boa into the *reject* pile. "He wouldn't do something like that, would he?"

"I have no idea. But I can't rule it out, either."

"Come on, let's think this through. If Dash bought the earrings for someone else, then why didn't he just hide them from you? Even if the box had accidently fallen on the floor, he still left it out in the open where you could see it." She cocked her head. "Where's the logic in that?"

"There isn't any, I guess. But if the earrings were for a friend's wife, then why wouldn't he just tell me his friend's name? Why was he being so secretive?"

"I understand your fear, honestly I do. But before you jump to any more conclusions, is there any way that we can investigate his story and see if it checks out?"

"Short of following him on Friday, I don't see

how." I breathed in my pain. "That part of what he said sounded true. That he really does have plans that night. Maybe he'll be seeing the woman he bought the earrings for." I searched her gaze, my pulse skittering. "If I took the chance and followed him, would you come with me?"

"Yes, of course. I wouldn't want you doing something like that alone."

"Thank you." I'd rejected Dash's proposal, but we'd agreed to keep seeing each other. It wasn't as if we've ended our affair or voided our agreement to remain monogamous to each other. But now I couldn't ignore the gut-clenching possibility that he could be sneaking around with someone else. "I appreciate you being here for me."

"Always." She closed the boa box. "I've never followed anyone before. Have you?"

"No. But I think we can do this. Dash said that his friend lives in a suburb just south of the city, and if that's where he's going, he won't be able to take the back roads to get there. He'll have to take the highway, which will work in our favor. I'll rent a car that he won't recognize, and we'll park on a turnout on the highway and wait until his truck or Zeke's SUV passes." I continued outlining the plan as it came together in my mind. "The party is supposed to be at seven. We should start our watch early to give ourselves plenty of time to look for him."

Alice appeared to be contemplating it all. "If

Zeke is driving, he'll notice if we get too close. He's trained to spot that sort of thing."

"We'll just have to be as careful as we can. We should probably disguise our appearances, too."

"It sounds so covert." She furrowed her brow. "But if Dash really is going out that night, and we manage to follow him to someone's house, what are you going to do once we get there?"

"I just want to drive by and see if there's a party going on. I think that kind of activity will be obvious." I glanced at the fancy feathers on the bed. "There would be other cars parked on the street and other people going in and out. Dash wouldn't be the only guest."

"You're right. I just hope that we can pull this off and get to the bottom of things."

"Me, too." I needed to know what was going on, and I wasn't going to rest until I found out.

"You look pretty as a blonde," Alice said, as we sat in the economy car I'd rented, waiting on the turnout on the highway near Dash's house and keeping our eye out for him.

"Thanks, but I don't feel very pretty." I was too anxious to think about anything except the cars going by. We'd been here for about thirty minutes so far.

I glanced over at Alice, and she fingered the ends of her short, spiky brown wig. We'd chosen styles that mimicked our own hair, except in different colors.

I fidgeted in my seat. "It's all so crazy. Me chasing down a man who doesn't even love me."

She hesitated for a second. "What if he does love you?"

"What?" I gaped at her. Had she lost her mind?

"I know it's a weird thing for me to say, especially now. But as badly as he wants to marry you, it's starting to make me wonder if he might love you and not even know it. People can block out those types of feelings."

"Is he blocking out that he's lying to me, too?"

"We don't know that he's lying. And we don't really know what's going on inside of him, either. Spencer struggled with his feelings. He didn't realize that he loved me until we were in the midst of a crisis."

"That's not the same as what's happening between me and Dash." I leaned forward, watching the highway.

"I'm sorry. I just—"

"There they are!" I exclaimed, as Zeke's SUV cruised past us. I recognized the car, but I knew the license plate number, too. "It's definitely them!"

"Then hurry up. Get out there."

"I can't just peel out onto the road." As jittery as I was, I felt as if I was learning to drive all over again. "Keep your eye on them, and I'll try to do this calmly."

"Okay." Alice stared out the windshield.

I merged onto the highway and stayed about three car lengths behind them, in the lane next to theirs. I'd prepared for this jaunt, reading tons of articles on how to tail someone and stay within surveillance range without being detected. Of course, none of those articles pertained to a situation like this, where the driver of the other vehicle was your celebrity lover's bodyguard.

"You're doing good," Alice said.

I maintained the speed limit, trying not to hyperventilate, my breathing coming in short, quick pants. I couldn't remember ever being this nervous, not even the first time I'd performed in public, and I'd gotten terrible stage fright that day.

What if I was wrong and Alice was right? What if Dash wasn't lying? Or cheating? And what if he really did love me?

No, no, no, I thought. I couldn't let my heart go there. I just needed to stay focused and follow him.

"Are you sure Dash is even in the car?" Alice asked. "I can't see him."

"He rides in back, where the windows are tinted really dark." I gripped the steering wheel, and we continued on our trek, my nerves in knots.

About twenty minutes later, Alice said, "You better change lanes. They're getting ready to turn onto the next highway."

"Which way?"

"Left. He's got his blinker on."

I merged into the lane where I needed to be. Luckily the Honda in front of me was turning, too, keeping a space between us. But once we made another turn farther on, I had to be more careful. By now, we were in a posh suburban neighborhood with less traffic and fewer places to hide.

I tried to stay as far back as I could, without losing sight of them. Finally, they turned onto another street that led to a small hill, and I drove straight past it.

Alice bobbed in her seat. "What are you doing?"

"I'm going to circle back. I don't want Zeke to see us turning right behind him."

"I hope we don't lose them."

"I don't think we will." I gestured toward the hill. "It looks like there aren't that many houses up there."

"Maybe you should have been a spy instead of a singer."

Yeah, I thought. Maybe I should've, considering the demise of my music career. Not that I'd had much time to focus on it lately. Between my dad's illness and my affair with Dash, I'd gotten sidetracked. But I still planned to keep pursuing it, putting more music out there on my own.

I waited a few minutes before I made a U-turn and came back around, creeping along the incline Zeke had driven up earlier.

Alice leaned forward, looking out her window. "I don't see the SUV. But you were right about it being less populated up here. There are only a few streets where they could've turned, and the one at the very top looks like a dead end."

I drove up and down the streets. The houses were few and far between, and the SUV wasn't parked in front of any of them.

"Maybe he pulled into a garage," Alice said.

Had I made a mistake by not following closer? "We still need to check the houses all the way at the top."

"Then let's go."

There was only one house at the top, and sure enough, we'd hit our mark. The SUV was parked in the driveway behind an iron fence.

"There's no party here," I said, my heart going numb. "Look how quiet it is."

"Watch out. The bodyguard's coming." Alice motioned with her chin. Zeke had just gotten out of the SUV and was striding toward the gate.

"I'll just act like I made a wrong turn." I looped the car around and retreated to the street directly below. I parked in front of a colonial-style house on the corner and caught my breath.

"Do you think he recognized us?" she asked.

"With these wigs? I don't know." I fought the urge to cry. "It doesn't matter to me if he did. It's over. I'm done. I don't ever want to see or speak to Dash again."

Alice put her hand on my knee. "Do you think we should wait a bit before you start despising Dash? It's only a little after seven. People are notoriously late to parties."

"Meaning what? That Dash was the first to arrive?"

"Don't you want to know for sure? I know it scared us when Zeke reacted the way he did, but maybe he thought we were party guests and was going to open the gate for us."

Should I let Alice be my voice of reason? From our vantage point, we would be able to tell if any other cars drove up the hill. I caved in, and we waited.

Twenty minutes. Then thirty. We even pushed it to forty, and the only vehicle that passed us was a white BMW. But it pulled into a garage on the street we were on.

With my pain growing every minute we waited, I finally asked, "Can we give up this charade now and accept that Dash lied?"

"Yes." Alice's voice was deflated. "I'm so sorry. You deserve better than this."

"Yes, I do. And you know what? I'm not going to curl up in a ball like one of those little pill bugs. I'm going to confront Dash. Now. Tonight." Preparing to do battle, I removed my wig, pulled off the nylon cap beneath it and tugged at the pins. Once my hair was free, I fluffed it around my shoulders. "How do I look?"

"Like a force to be reckoned with." Alice got rid of her wig, too.

I zoomed back up the hill, adrenaline pumping through my veins. As bold as could be, I barreled straight ahead, blocking the gate in front of the house.

"Here we go," Alice said, as she watched the bodyguard stomp toward us. "Damn, but he's big."

"Not as big as I am right now." I shut off the engine and swung open my door.

I heard Zeke cuss before he asked, "Tracy, what are you doing here?"

"You didn't suspect that the blonde who made the wrong turn was me?" I grabbed the wig from the console and threw it at the gate. When it landed on the ground, the poor thing looked like roadkill. "Who lives here? Who is Dash with?"

"Just calm down and go home."

I glared at him. "I'm not going anywhere."

Zeke removed his phone from his pocket. Was he calling the police to report me for harassment? No way, I thought. He couldn't do that, not without creating a PR nightmare for Dash.

"Are you warning him that I'm here?" I asked.

"Yes, I am." He fired off a text.

I looked over my shoulder at Alice, and she opened her door.

"Is everything all right?" she asked me.

"It's fine," I assured her. I gazed pointedly at Zeke. "I'm not leaving until Dash comes outside."

Zeke's phone beeped, and my pulse jumped.

He glanced at the screen. "Dash says that he'll talk to you later, after you go home."

"I want to talk to him now," I countered.

Zeke shook his head. "Just go, Tracy."

"And let him finish his rendezvous with another woman? Screw you and screw him, too."

Zeke shook his head. "You're mixing everything up."

"Oh yeah? Then tell Dash to unmix it for me." I

glanced at Alice again. She shielded herself with the passenger door, as if she was expecting a shootout. I stood out in the open, wearing my rage on my sleeve and welcoming whatever bullets came my way.

Zeke exchanged a few more texts with Dash, and my lying, cheating lover came outside. He looked angry. But I was fuming mad, too. What was that old saying, something about hell having no fury like a woman scorned?

Zeke unlocked the gate, and Dash approached me. Alice watched us for a second then slipped back inside the car and closed her door—giving me the privacy I needed to lay into Dash. Zeke backed off, too, and headed over to his SUV.

Dash grabbed my hand and pulled me toward the edge of the road. I yanked my hand away and met his gaze head on.

"I'm not with another woman," he all but growled.

"Then what's the deal with those earrings?" I snapped back. "And whose house is this?"

"I rented it for my mom, and I bought the earrings for her."

I flinched, shocked into silence.

"I got her a bunch of other gifts, too," he said. "I'm giving her all the stuff you won't let me buy for you."

I found my voice, hard and quick. "Don't use me as your excuse to buy things for her." I wasn't to blame for that. "How long has she even been back in your life?"

He told me the entire Lola story, and my heart hurt

for him. He was letting his mother take advantage of his success and use him for his money. I glanced at the house and spotted a willowy figure peering out the window. She was watching us.

"Come with me," I said. "Leave her behind and come home with me."

"Seriously? After you accused me of cheating on you? I would have never done something like that."

"I was confused and hurt, Dash. I suspected that you were lying to me about the earrings, and I over-reacted. But I've been struggling the whole time we've been together. I wanted to have an affair with you because I thought that if I slept with you, I could get some of my power back."

"What are you talking about?"

I forged ahead, forcing myself to say the words I knew he wouldn't want to hear. "I've never stopped loving you. Even after all the years we've been apart, my feelings never really changed."

He stepped back, away from the streetlight and into a haze of darkness. "You love me? But you've been lying to me and pretending that you don't?"

"I was trying not to love you, but it didn't work. Then I started hoping and praying that you'd love me, too. But you didn't, even though you asked me to marry you. Everything we've been doing has been a mess."

"You're right. It's a total mess. At least with my mom, I know where I stand."

I ached for him. And for myself, too. "She's just going to hurt you again."

"Not if I keep giving her the things she wants."

His reasoning made me even sadder than I already was. "I'm sorry that I accused you of being with someone else. I should've had more faith in you. But it's hard, loving someone who doesn't love me back."

"You know I'm not capable of that."

"Alice thinks you could be." My voice cracked. "Earlier, before we followed you here, she said that you could be blocking your feelings."

His voice was shaky, too. "I'm not blocking anything. I've always known that love was difficult for me, and I never denied that it started when I was a kid."

"With an emptiness your mother created." And now she was back, pulling his strings, treating him like a puppet. "I wanted to fix you the first time we were together. But my heart got crushed instead."

"And now I crushed it again." He moved closer to me. "We have to end it. We have to stop the cycle."

I lifted my hand to skim his jaw. "Maybe if we…"

"No." His expression went blank. "I can't be what you need, Tracy. I don't have it in me."

I lowered my hand. Touching him would only make the pain worse. "I'm going to go." I couldn't stay another minute, immersed in this kind of torture. "I won't ever bother you again."

He didn't say anything. He just stood in the shadows while I walked to the car, my footsteps echoing in the night.

I got behind the wheel, and Alice turned to face me. We didn't speak. I waited until I turned off his mother's street before I pulled over and burst into tears.

Crying over the man I still loved.

Twelve

Dash

I strode past Zeke, and he closed the gate, leaving me to my misery. He didn't expect me to confide in him. I wouldn't have, anyway. Losing Tracy was my pain to bear.

I returned to the house, and Mom rushed over to me with a dramatic flair. "Who was that girl?"

"No one." I made a beeline for the bar and poured myself a vodka on the rocks. I swigged it, letting it burn its way down my throat.

"She must've been someone to have upset you this way."

I didn't respond. I was an emotional wreck, torn

apart by everything Tracy had said. That she'd never stopped loving me. That her heart was still yearning for mine. On top of that, I had to contend with Alice's disturbing opinion of me. The bit about me blocking my feelings and being in love, too, as if I was too scared or stupid to know the difference.

I wasn't stupid. But I'd always been afraid of getting too close, of repeating the mistake my dad had made with my mom, of needing someone so badly that you destroyed yourself over it. I didn't want to lose my soul to love. I was supposed to be immune to that. I'd done everything in my power to protect myself from it.

I frowned at my mom. She sat on the sofa and fingered the new Gucci jewels at her ears. The earrings I'd lied to Tracy about. But she'd lied to me, too, deceiving me about the nature of our affair.

"I wish you'd tell me what's going on, Dash."

"There's nothing to tell." It seemed as if my whole world was crumbling, yet I still had my money, my career and my mansion. The things I'd wanted to share with Tracy.

Did I love her? The thought panicked me. I felt the sheer terror washing over my bones. I'd spent my entire adulthood dismissing love, and now I was drowning in the sudden fear of it.

But what did love feel like? How would I know for sure? This had already been one of the worst nights of my life, and it was getting more chaotic by the second.

The uncertainty. The agony. The pounding of my heart.

Mom studied me. "You look positively miserable. Do you want to finish eating? Will that help?"

I glanced at our leftover dinner on the table. Roasted chicken and all the fixings. We'd been in the middle of it when Zeke had texted, alerting me that Tracy was outside. And now she was gone. I'd sent her away for good.

"I'm not hungry anymore," I replied. My stomach would cramp if I took even one more bite.

"Should we stream some music?"

I shook my head. "There's nothing I want to hear."

She gestured to the TV. "A movie, then?"

"I don't want to watch anything, either."

"Is there anything I can do to help?"

"No." But I was surprised by what sounded like genuine concern on her part. Or as close to genuine as she knew how to be. I studied her, then asked, "Why didn't you ever love my dad the way he loved you?"

She flinched. "What does that have to do with anything?"

"I just want to know, that's all." Love was the issue of the night, the word spinning around in my head. The emotion I couldn't seem to face.

She frowned and replied, "Relationships have always been hard for me." She fidgeted in her seat. "Some bad things happened to me when I was young, and I've just never been able to…"

Her words trailed off, and I realized how messed up she really was. Not that I hadn't always known it. But something seemed different this time. Or maybe I was just getting a better understanding of her, based on how messed up I was, too.

She fingered her earrings again. "I appreciate everything you're doing for me, Dash. Renting me this house and buying me gifts."

"I know." She equated love with material things, and she'd taught me to have that mindset, too.

"You're a good son," she said. "The best."

"Thank you." It was easy being the type of son she wanted, now that I had the means to please her. But I wasn't the best boyfriend or lover or whatever to Tracy. I couldn't give her anything that would validate me in her eyes.

No, that wasn't true. If I let myself, I could give Tracy the very thing she wanted most.

For me to love her.

The next few days were a living hell. Thoughts of Tracy consumed me, every moment of every hour. But I was still scared, panicked beyond belief.

I sat on my porch steps, waiting for Zeke. I'd asked him to come by and talk. I couldn't confide in my mom. She didn't have a normal understanding of love. My only option was Zeke. Plus, he was the only person I could spill my guts to who wasn't part of Tracy's camp. My dad was gone, and Pop was *her* dad. I couldn't tell him how I was feeling, not without involving Tracy. Spencer would be a problem, too. He was Alice's husband, and Alice was Tracy's best friend. Everyone was just too connected.

Zeke showed up with a troubled expression on his roughly chiseled face. He sat beside me and said, "Are you sure there isn't anyone else you want to have this conversation with?"

"Yeah, I'm sure."

He frowned. "I probably won't be very good at offering you advice."

I handed him a longneck beer. I'd barely touched mine. "You can't be any worse at this than I am."

He accepted the drink. "Don't bet on it."

I studied him. He wasn't wearing his customary suit. This was his day off, and he was in regular clothes: shorts, flip-flops and a Polynesian-print shirt. The other security guys filled in for him when he wasn't working, but I didn't need a bodyguard at the moment. I needed a friend. Either way, Zeke wouldn't be around forever. At some point, he would return to the corporate side of his business and assign another bodyguard to me.

I didn't know much about his personal life. But when I first hired him and his crew, he'd told me that he'd been raised in a house as big as mine. Zeke came from a successful Hollywood family, only he preferred to keep a low profile.

"Did you love your ex-wife?" I asked.

He winced a little. "What kind of question is that?"

"I just want to know if you've ever been in love. Like, really, deeply in love."

"Yeah, I have. And, yeah, it was with my ex."

I kept studying him, analyzing him. For now, it was easier than analyzing myself. "What happened? Why aren't you still together?"

"It was complicated." He swigged his beer. "Too complicated for me to get into. But it still affects me and how I live my life now."

I respected his right to be vague. But I still needed to hash out my problems. "What does it feel like?"

He gave me a disturbed look. "To get divorced?"

I shook my head. "To be in love."

"It feels like someone's sitting on your chest, smothering the crap out of you. But it feels amazing, too, when it's going right. All you want is to be with that person."

"I've always wanted to be with Tracy. Even the years we weren't together, I couldn't shake her from my blood. But I couldn't accept that she loved me, and I couldn't…"

"Love her back?"

I nodded. "In my family, love was a word associated with pain, a word that was used to manipulate and destroy. I watched my dad wither away because of it, and I vowed that I'd never let that happen to me."

"Love isn't supposed to destroy people. That's not how it's intended to work. Plenty of people have healthy, loving relationships."

I shot him a curious glance. "See, you are good at this."

He shrugged. "It's just common sense."

"Not to someone like me. Look what I'm doing with my mom. She abandoned me, and now I'm giving her everything she wants and trying to make her love me."

"Old wounds run deep."

"That's for sure. I've been going out of my way to buy my mom's affection, yet I've been denying Tracy what she wants."

"Those two women couldn't be more opposite."

I nodded and gazed out at the lake, knowing it was time to stop being afraid and admit the truth. That I'd always loved Tracy, even if I'd buried those feelings in the deepest, darkest part of me. I'd allowed my mother's rejection to ruin what I could've had with Tracy. What I still could have. Love wasn't the enemy. It could be my salvation, if I let it be.

Dear God, I thought. How easy was that? The burden I'd been carrying around had just been lifted from my shoulders.

But within seconds, my confidence fell, and a different kind of fear slammed through me. What if it was too late to win Tracy back? What if I'd hurt her too badly?

"I have to apologize for something," Zeke said suddenly.

I blinked at him. "I'm sorry. What?"

"I should have been more alert that night. I didn't

have a clue that Tracy and Alice were following us. They outsmarted me, and I didn't catch on until it was too late." He shook his head. "I screwed up, and you paid the price."

"That isn't true. I got exactly what I deserved. Besides, if Tracy hadn't shown up, I probably never would've told her about my mom." But I didn't want to hide anything from Tracy anymore. No matter what mistakes I'd made, I needed to lay my heart on the line. And hope that she still loved me enough to take me back.

I stood on Tracy's front porch, in the dark, a black cowboy hat shielding my eyes. I'd driven myself here, all alone with my hopes and dreams and fears.

I pressed the buzzer, with my pulse thudding in my throat. I heard someone approach the door but it didn't open. Was that Tracy? Was she peering out the peephole? As far as I could tell, she was by herself. I didn't see any other cars in the driveway.

The door creaked open, and Tracy gazed at me through the crack. "What are you doing here?"

"I just want to talk." And ask her to marry me, I thought. I had a ring burning a hole in my pocket. A diamond I'd chosen with love and care. But would she accept my proposal? Would I be able to prove myself to her?

She invited me in, and I followed her into the house. Her living room was tidy, and there was a scented candle burning on the coffee table. Strawberry or cherry or something. She looked soft and pretty, and I longed to touch her, to skim my hand against hers, but I kept my distance.

"Can I get you anything?" she asked.

"No, thank you." She seemed leery of me. But I couldn't blame her. If I were her, I'd be cautious, too.

"Do you want to sit?" She gestured to the sofa.

I nodded and removed my hat, placing it on the coffee table. I glanced at the Home Sweet Home pillow propped up at one end of the couch and imagined her bringing it to Pine Tower if she moved in with me. But this wasn't going well so far. She sat in a chair on the other side of the room, as far away from me as possible, putting an even bigger gap between us.

I was so nervous that I barely knew where to start. I ran a hand through my hair. "I'm sorry about the way things ended. I never should have lied to you. I handled everything badly."

"You came to apologize?"

"Yes, but I have so much more to say, to tell you." I kept my gaze riveted to hers. "I love you, Tracy. I'm madly, achingly in love with you."

She gasped. "But you never were before. You—"

"I know the difference now." I tapped on my chest, in the vicinity of my heart. "I've always felt it, this heaviness inside of me. What Alice said was true. I've loved you all along without recognizing it. Even the years we've been apart, I couldn't get you out of my mind. I watched your career rise and fall, and then when I became successful, all I wanted was to see you again. To try to record with you, to do whatever it took to be around you." I stood and moved away from the couch. "You were right to turn down my other proposal and not be interested in a ring from me. But I needed to get you one this time." I removed the case from my pocket and flipped it open.

She got up and walked over to where I was. She stared at the diamond, as if it was blinding her. Was it too big? Too showy? Had I chosen the wrong style?

"It's heart-shaped," she said.

My breath rushed out. "I wanted it to represent what I should've given you years ago. My heart. My love. My life."

Tears flooded her eyes. Was that a good sign?

I hurriedly said, "You don't have to sing with me or do anything that doesn't feel right to you. It's going to be hard to avoid the press, though, and I'm hoping that if you agree to marry me, you'll be okay with everyone knowing that we're together. I'd be happy to tell the world that we're engaged. I want nothing more than for you to become my wife."

"I've waited a lifetime for you to love me, to want me in this way." She searched my gaze, long and deep. "But are you sure you're not acting on impulse? Or that the decision isn't going to overwhelm you later?"

"I'm positive. But I can't sugarcoat it or promise

that everything will be perfect, and especially now that my mom is back in the picture."

"That does present a troubling picture, but it's okay. It's not your fault."

I set the ring next to my hat on the coffee table, letting the diamond shine on its own. "At least our kids won't have to go through what I went through." I moved closer, desperate to touch her. "Marry me, Tracy, and be the mother of my children." I put my hand on her stomach, splaying my fingers across it. "We can't bring back the one we lost, but we can have lots of other babies."

"Oh, my God, no." She stepped out of reach. "I love you, Dash. But I can't do this." She gazed at me with pain in her eyes. "I can't marry you, not if…"

Dumbstruck, I merely stared at her. "You don't want to create a family with me?"

"Yes, I want to, more than you can possibly know." She clutched her middle. "But there's a secret I've been keeping, something that I should have told you long before now."

Thirteen

Tracy

I walked over to the sofa and sat down, inviting Dash to join me. This wasn't a conversation I wanted to have standing in the middle of the room. Truthfully, it wasn't something I wanted to discuss at all. But Dash had just asked me to have his babies.

The thought made me ache—in my heart, in my womb.

Once we were settled beside each other, I said, "It's extremely unlikely that I'll ever be able to get pregnant again. I have a condition that..."

Dash watched me with a concerned expression. "What is it, Tracy? What's wrong?"

"It's called premature ovarian failure. It's when the ovaries quit working before the age of forty. I'm taking hormones and vitamins, but there's no treatment that can restore it." I explained further, getting it all out there, even as personal as it was. "I still have occasional periods, but they're few and far between. At some point, they're going to stop altogether." I blinked back my tears. "I haven't told anyone about this except for Alice."

Dash frowned. "Your dad doesn't know?"

"I didn't want to worry him, especially when he had such a health scare of his own. I didn't see the point in telling you, either. You and I were just having an affair. There was no future between us. But now…" I rocked forward.

"It's okay," he said softly. "This doesn't change anything for me. I love you, and I want to spend the rest of my life with you."

I looked into his eyes. "But you just said before that you wanted me to be the mother of your children."

He reached for my hand. "There are other ways to have a family. We could adopt or use a surrogate or donor eggs or whatever else people do these days. But only if you'd be comfortable with any of that. If not, we don't have to have kids. It can be just us."

My heart clenched. "I want children, I absolutely do. But this condition just makes me feel so inadequate, as if I'm less of a woman, as if I failed somehow."

"That's not true. You're still the same person you always were, and I'd be lucky to have you."

"But I'm still hurting that our first baby was taken away."

"I know. I'm still hurting over that, too. I have so many regrets from the past. And now, seeing you like this… I'm so sorry for everything you're going through. I wish I could make it better."

"My doctor has been encouraging me to join a support group." I took a shaky breath. "Maybe I should do that. Maybe it would help."

"If partners are allowed to attend or sit in on some of the meetings, I'll go with you…if you want me there."

Suddenly, the tears I'd been fighting broke free and I burst out crying. Dash was doing and saying everything right, but by now, my emotions were spent.

He leaned toward me, and I latched on to him, bawling in his arms. He held me tight and close, comforting me the best he could. I glanced at the coffee table where he'd left the engagement ring he'd chosen for me.

The heart. The diamond.

He stroked my hair, and I put my head against his chest and listened to the beats of his heart.

So steady, so real.

I cuddled closer, drawing from his strength, from his love, from how much I loved him. Finally,

I stopped crying and sat forward, catching the last of my shaky breaths.

"Are you okay?" he asked. "Is there anything I can do?"

"I'll be fine." I got up to get a box of tissues, drying my face and wiping my runny nose. "But there is something you can do that will make a difference."

"Anything, Tracy. Just tell me what it is."

"Ask me to marry you again."

He gazed longingly at me, then picked up the ring. When he got down on bended knee, my heart fluttered.

"Will you do me the honor of becoming my wife?" he asked. "Will you share my home with me? Will you be my partner in every way?"

"Yes," I eagerly replied. I couldn't wait for us to start our life together, to make the best of whatever the universe had in store for us. He put the ring on my finger, and as the diamond caught the light, I saw hope in each and every facet. "Look at that. I'm wearing your heart."

He returned to his feet. "It's always going to belong to you. But I wish I'd given it to you a long time ago."

"I have it now, and that's all that matters." I wasn't going to dwell on the pain from the past, not anymore.

We kissed soft and slow, sealing our commitment, taking time to savor it.

After two or three more kisses, he said, "Thank

you for loving me all these years. I never understood how important that was. Or how much I needed it."

I met his gaze. "You're welcome. But we still have a long road ahead of us, with announcing our engagement to the press, with me trying to rebuild my career, with our options for having a family. There's a lot to think about."

He nodded. "I still have to deal with my mom, too."

I reached out to hug him, comforting him in the way he'd done with me earlier. "Don't worry, Dash. I'll help you face that challenge." I nuzzled the side of his face, letting a bit of his beard stubble abrade me. "No matter what happens, we'll always be in this together."

After a bout of sweet silence, I led Dash to my room, wanting him in my bed. Right now, newly engaged, with his ring on my finger.

"It's been a while since we did this," I said, moving closer to him, inhaling the scent of his skin, of his clothes, of his cologne, of everything that was part of him. "We haven't made love since before the barbecue at your house."

He met my gaze. "I missed you, even when everything was falling apart."

"Me, too." I would never doubt or distrust him again.

He started undressing me, removing my blouse and putting his glorious hands on me. He divested me of my bra and peeled off my jeans, running his thumb along the elastic waistband of my plain white panties. I didn't want to turn the lights off in the room. I liked that he was looking at me, seeing all of me.

"We don't have to use protection. You know, since we don't really need it," I said. "Besides, I want to feel you inside me without anything between us." No barriers, I thought. Just him and me.

"I'll do whatever you want. But I think I should make you come first."

He dropped onto his knees, and I latched on to his shoulders. He'd already proposed to me in this position, and now he was sliding my panties down my legs...

Down and down...

All the way off...

He used his mouth, doing wicked things to me with his tongue, and I swayed on my feet. I felt as if I'd loved him for centuries. My fiancé. My future husband.

He worked his magic, my skin tingling, my sex going damp. As excitement pitched low in my belly, he used slow, deliberate strokes, making me sigh, making me moan.

I watched him with breathless anticipation.

He looked so strong and handsome and wild, bringing me closer and closer to a climax. He made a pleasured sound, and I got even more aroused. He was enjoying this as much as I was.

I wanted to tell him how good it felt, how he was doing everything right, but by now I was beyond words.

I merely shuddered and convulsed against his face.

He remained on his knees, teasing me, nuzzling me. It was sweet, sweet sin. Could I be any warmer? Any stickier?

Finally, he stood and kissed me on the mouth, intensifying the moment. I leaned against him, breathless once again.

Soon, he yanked off his boots, and I helped him get naked, tugging at his shirt and unzipping his jeans.

He backed me against the bed, and we tumbled onto it, falling down together.

I used my hands, making him fully erect. Then, wanting more, I slid down his body and swirled my tongue around the salty tip of him. His abs flexed, and I took him all the way into my mouth. He let me do as I pleased. For a while, anyway.

When he couldn't take it anymore, he made me stop.

He climbed on top of me, and we stared into each other's eyes. He entered me, and I lifted my hips, taking him deeper, relishing the feeling of having him inside me, of being this close. We moved in unison, thrusting in the same passionate rhythm. I wrapped my legs around him, holding him strong and tight. He rubbed his cheek against mine, making me warm and woozy.

He increased the tempo, and I arched my body, bending myself to his will.

In the next pivotal moment, I came in a burst of need, catching my breath with every hot, slick spasm.

With a look of sexy concentration on his brow, Dash followed me, his muscles bunching, his arms straining above me.

I closed my eyes as he came, so glad that he was mine.

After the sex, we stayed in bed, indulging in cookie dough ice cream from the carton, passing it back and forth and licking the spoon clean. I'd been eating ice cream every night since we split up, drowning myself in sadness, and now I was celebrating.

Dash said, "I think you should move in with me before we announce our engagement. Otherwise, the press is going to bang down your door, trying to get pictures and interviews. At least at my place, you'll be behind a security gate."

"It's going to be crazy, having people take an interest in me like that." I'd never been at that level of fame before. "But I'm excited about moving in with you."

"Then will you pack some bags and move in with me tonight? I can arrange for the rest of your stuff to be trucked over later."

"That sounds good to me." I wanted to spend all my days and nights with him. The sooner, the better.

"I'll call a Realtor and put my house on the market. I'll quit the feedstore, too." I couldn't work a public job and be married to him, not without his fans tracking me down there. "But I'll keep doing my VA stuff until my house sells and I have some extra money of my own."

"You can work in whatever capacity you want, but I think you should focus on your music. I won't keep bugging you about the duet, though. You can take everything at your own pace."

I looked into his dark, sexy eyes. "I'm going to do whatever I can to rebuild my career, but I want to sign a prenup, Dash. I don't want any part of this marriage to be about your money."

He shook his head. "You really are stubborn about that, aren't you?"

"It'll make me feel better to know that I'm earning my own keep."

"I'm not going to fight you on your independence. I have faith in you and your career. But if you want my help, I'll always be ready and willing."

"Thank you." I watched him take a bite of the ice cream. "Speaking of money, what's the next step with your mom?"

He sighed. "I don't know. But honestly, I think she could benefit by getting some help."

"You mean therapy?"

He nodded. "The last time I saw her, I asked her about my dad, and she mentioned how hard it was for her to love him because of some bad stuff that happened to her when she was young."

"When she was in foster care?"

"She didn't specify, but that's my assumption."

"Do you want to continue having a relationship with her?" I needed to know how he truly felt.

"Yes, I do. But I can't just keep buying her things to win her affection. I want her to learn to care for me in a deeper way."

"Do you think she's capable of that?"

He nodded. "She seemed genuinely concerned for me when I was upset over you."

"Then you should talk to her about getting counseling, so she can explore those feelings. Plus, she needs to try to heal from whatever happened to her when she was young. Maybe you could even do family therapy at some point."

"That's definitely something to consider." He smiled a little nervously as me. "It wouldn't hurt for me to face my childhood issues, all that crap I've been carrying around. But I'm not sure how receptive she's going to be about seeing someone."

"Can I go with you when you talk to her?" I asked.

"Yes, of course. But are you sure you're up for it?"

"Absolutely. We're in this together, remember?" I intended to stand by his side in every way I could.

As soon as Dash and I entered his mother's house, I could tell that she was threatened by me. But I'd expected as much. She wasn't the type to welcome another female into her lair.

Dash introduced her as Lola, and when she reached out to shake my hand, she tilted her head at a haughty angle. I'd never seen a picture of her when she was younger, so I didn't know what she looked like before, but she fit what I'd imagined her to be. Along with her false eyelashes and bloodred nails, she had a trim figure and short auburn hair, styled just so. She sported an elegant dress and stately heels, a designer outfit Dash had purchased for her, no doubt. She'd paired her ensemble with several pieces of fine jewelry. Again, things that must have come from Dash.

Within seconds, she caught sight of the ring on my finger, staring blatantly at it.

Dash spoke up and said, "Tracy is my fiancée, Mom. We just got engaged a few days ago."

"Is that so?" Lola raised her delicately arched brows at me. "Aren't you the one who was here last week causing a scene?"

"Yes, that was me," I replied. "But it was just a misunderstanding, and we worked things out."

"A five-carat misunderstanding," she quipped, accurately assessing the size of my diamond.

I moved closer to Dash, standing near him, supporting him. We'd already told my dad we were engaged, and he was thrilled for us. Pop had even cried a little, telling me how happy and proud my mother would've been. But all Lola seemed to noticed was the value of my ring. Was it going to be possible for this woman to become a better person? Heavens, I hoped so.

She turned to Dash and asked, "Are you sure you aren't rushing into anything?"

"I'm positive." He reached for my hand. "I've loved Tracy for years. I just had a tough time accepting it."

She paused, as if she was deciding what to say next. Was she worried that if she didn't start reacting favorably to his news, he would stop buying her pretty things?

She chirpily said, "Let's celebrate your engagement with some champagne." She strutted over to the bar, her heels clicking on the hardwood floors. "I'll put a bottle of Dom on ice."

Dash glanced at me, and I shrugged. We had time for a drink. We were here to discuss an important issue, to hopefully change the course of all of our lives.

While the champagne chilled, we gathered in the living room. "This is a lovely house," I said.

"Yes, it is," Lola replied. She smiled a bit too adoringly at her son. A second later, she spoke directly to him. "Dash knows how much it means to me."

He returned her smile, and once the champagne was chilled, she popped the cork and poured it into three crystal flutes. She gave us ours and raised hers in the air. "To the happy couple," she said.

We all clinked glasses, toasting the moment. A moment that wouldn't last. I doubted that Lola was going to be happy when she learned what our agenda was.

"We need to talk, Mom," Dash said.

"About what?" she asked, gazing at her drink.

"About coping with the past."

She whipped her head up. "What?"

"I think it would be beneficial for you to see a psychologist and work through the stuff that happened to you when you were young. And then maybe later, we can get therapy together."

"Oh, my goodness." Her breath rushed out. "It's been too long, too much time for that kind of nonsense."

"There's nothing wrong with getting help," I said, inserting myself into the discussion.

She quickly argued, "But things are fine the way they are. Dash is happy now." She turned to him. "Look how good everything is for you. You have an outstanding career, and you're engaged to be married."

"Yes, but my relationship with you isn't normal, Mom. I want more out of it than just buying you fancy gifts."

"But the gifts are nice," she countered.

Was she afraid of facing her past and having to learn to be the kind of mother her son needed?

"Just give the therapy a try," he said.

"If I say no, are you going to cut me off?" she asked.

He set his champagne aside. "You mean quit paying your way? I'm not here to blackmail you. But if you're not willing to see things my way, then maybe you should get a job and support yourself."

"A job? See, you really are blackmailing me. This is awful." Lola's voice quavered. "Just awful."

By now, she was playing the drama queen and trying to make Dash feel sorry for her. But he wasn't having it.

He kept his cool, even when she heaved a big woeful sigh. Like the heroine of an old movie on the verge of a fainting spell.

Fourteen

Dash

"I can't work," my mother said, pleading with me to let her off the hook. I figured that between getting therapy and getting a job, she would've chosen the therapy, but she wasn't agreeing to either.

What an ordeal. I glanced over at Tracy, appreciating that she was here with me. That'd she'd agreed to be my wife. That she loved me in a way that people were meant to be loved. My mixed-up mom didn't have a clue what that meant.

"Why can't you work?" I asked her.

"Because…" She lowered herself onto the sofa, as if she was so distraught that she needed to sit and fan herself, using a piece of junk mail she'd left on the coffee table. "I don't have any job skills."

"I'm sure there's something you'd be good at," Tracy chimed in.

Mom shot her an annoyed look. "This isn't any of your business."

"Don't treat her that way," I snapped, coming to Tracy's defense. "She's only trying to help."

"But everything was fine before you got engaged. You weren't trying to get me into counseling then. You weren't saddling me with a job, either."

I sighed. "You can't just sit around here and do nothing." That wouldn't accomplish a danged thing.

"What's wrong with me being a lady of leisure?" she argued.

"A person has to do something of value," I responded. "Or at least have some goals."

"But I'm too old and ill equipped to work."

Who was she trying to kid? "You're smart as a whip and highly attractive, too. I'm sure you'd find something that you'd excel at."

Tracy said, "Maybe you could work at a jewelry store or at an upscale boutique."

Mom huffed out a breath. "I'm not working as a salesperson."

"I think you'd move onto a managerial position in no time," Tracy replied. "You could even take some online courses and get an education."

"I can't believe this." Mom quit slouching on the sofa. She stood and refilled her champagne, posing with the flute. "Look at me, Dash. I'm not the type who was meant to work. I'm not meant to be analyzed by some pesky psychologist, either."

"But you're the type who was meant to abandon your kid and then come back into his life when you found out that he's rich and successful?" I stared her down, hurt and frustrated that she was belittling our relationship and ignoring the way it should be.

She glared at me. "Is that what this is about? You're punishing me for the past?"

"It's not punishment. I'm a grown man who's finally learned how to give and receive and accept love." I squared my shoulders. "But I can't make things right with you until you're willing to try."

"So you're taking everything away from me instead?"

"I'm not taking anything away. I'm just asking you to make a change. I can't begin to fathom what you experienced when you were young, and I'm sorry for any pain it caused you. But I know what I endured, and how it affected me."

She glanced away, as if she was getting emotional. But a second later, she said, "You had a tough childhood, but look how charmed your life is now. You're a millionaire. You're probably even on your way to becoming a billionaire. I don't see the harm in you supporting me without any strings attached."

"I see plenty of harm in it. I spent my entire life feeling like trash and thinking that I had to be rich to matter." I glanced at Tracy. "She loved me when

I was poor, and she loves me now. My success has nothing to do with it."

Mom scowled. "But she's going to marry you, while I'm being forced to change my ways."

She sipped her champagne, a look of damnation on her face. "I should go to the press and tell them how utterly horrible you're being to me."

She was threatening me? No way, I thought. No effing way. "Do you honestly think that the public is going to side with you? What are you going to say that makes me sound so awful? That I'm trying to help you recover from your past? That I want us to attend family counseling, but you're refusing to go?" I wasn't going to back down, not now, not like this. "And just so you know, I have an entire PR team who manages my publicity, so if you go to the press, I'm going to fire back." For now, Tracy and I hadn't even announced our engagement yet. The last thing I needed was my mom doing it for us.

She clicked her shiny red nails on the bar top. "Your fans already know that I left when you were young, so why should I keep quiet? I might as well make my identity known."

"You don't care what people are going to think of you?" Tracy asked.

Mom shrugged. "Everyone already thinks I'm rotten, anyway." She paused, still clicking her nails. "In fact, I think we should all do a reality show together. The public would eat it up. Me as the glamorous villain, Dash as the world-famous artist and you as his love-is-everything fiancée or wife or whatever you'll be by then."

Tracy gaped at her. I did, too. Both of our mouths hung open.

Mom kept chattering. "You should talk to your agent about it, Dash. And then they can present it to whatever network they think will be interested. Who knows? There might even be a bidding war."

Holy cow, I thought. "I'm not making a TV show with you."

"But it's a way for all of us to be a family. And on top of that, it'll boost your fame and income, too. You'll be an even bigger star than you already are."

"I don't want to be that kind of star. And that's not my idea of being a family." I wanted something nice and nurturing and normal.

"Fine." She tossed back the rest of her champagne, all drama, all glamorous-villain. "I'll just have to get my own show. Or I'll join the cast of another show that's already established. I can still become a celebrity."

"You know what? You're right. You can do whatever you want." I wasn't going to worry about the repercussions her self-serving deeds would have on me. I was already in the spotlight, and once Tracy and I announced our engagement, she would be knee-deep in it, too. Fame was a part of our lives, either way. "I'm sure you'll find an agent to represent you once you tell them that you're related to me. But don't do it until after Tracy and I go public."

Mom frowned. "How long is that going to take?"

"It'll be sometime this week." We didn't want to drag things out any longer than necessary. "You won't have to wait long. Then you can have your life to yourself, just as long as you keep your distance from me and mine."

Mom moved away from me, and suddenly she seemed overwhelmed, as if being in a reality show wasn't such a great idea, after all. She paced the room, her shoes echoing on the hardwood floors.

Tap...tap...tap...

Was she having second thoughts about being excluded from my life? Was she afraid of being alone? Of being scorned and cast out?

She stopped and turned to me. "I'm sorry," she said shakily. "And I'm sorry for being rude to Tracy. I was just being obstinate, saying stupid things I didn't mean. I do care about what people think, and I especially don't want you to hate me."

"I don't hate you." I spoke quietly. "But you need help. You can't go around using people and treating them badly."

Her breath hitched. "I know."

"Does that mean you're willing to give the therapy a shot?"

"Yes, but it's going to be hard for me. I'm not comfortable talking about myself like that, rehashing everything from my past."

"I understand. But it's got to be done." One step at a time. I chanced a smile at her.

Tears gathered in her eyes. "Are you still going to support me? Or do you still want me to get a job?"

"I'll support you." But mostly I was going to support her in emotional ways. Someday, I hoped she would see the full benefit of that and would be there for me, too. For now, I wasn't expecting miracles. But at least this was a start.

My mother reached out to hug me, and I felt her tremble in my arms. I could sense Tracy watching us.

Afterward, I smiled at the woman I was going to marry, so damned grateful that I had her support. That she was my miracle. That she loved me, just as I loved her—with every beat of our hearts.

Tracy and I went home and made love, touching and kissing and breathing each other in. She sat naked on my lap, riding me, her body arched, her hair falling down her back. I watched the way she moved, thinking how perfect she was. I cupped her breasts in my hands, rubbing her nipples, making them hard.

As she stroked me with her wetness, with her sweet dampness, I imagined what our honeymoon night was going to be like. I had no idea if we would be in a glitzy hotel or a cabin in the mountains or a bungalow on a tropical island. I just knew that we would be together, giving each other pleasure.

I pictured her in a lace corset and thigh-high stockings, lovely little things she would've worn under her gown.

I envisioned flower petals, too, lots of them, in pretty colors, scattered on the bed.

"I'm thinking about our wedding night," I said, pulling her into my fantasy.

"You are?" Her gaze locked on to mine.

"Yeah." I lifted myself up to kiss her, hot and quick. "About how romantic the sex is going to be." I kissed her again. "Wild and romantic."

She sank deeper onto my lap, milking my body with hers. "Tell me more about it."

"You'd be riding me, like you are now, and there'd be flower petals everywhere."

"What kind?"

"Roses, and they'd smell really good and sweet." I circled her waist with my hands, helping her move up and down. "You'd be dressed in wedding-type lingerie, except with no panties."

She bit down on her bottom lip. "What would you be wearing?"

"A tuxedo shirt, that you ripped open. And my pants would be on the floor, with my jacket and tie and your gown."

She shivered on top of me, aroused by our conversation. "Would I be wearing a veil?"

"While we're in bed? Hell yeah." That added a new element to the fantasy. "One of those shorter ones that I could lift every time I kissed you."

"What about my gown on the floor? What does it look like?"

"It's long and silky with antique lace and those tiny buttons up the back."

"The old-fashioned kind that are covered in fabric?"

"Yes, ma'am. But I would get so impatient when I try to get you out of that dress, I'd destroy some of them."

She leaned over me, her hair falling across the sides of her face. "You'd be that anxious to be with me."

"I couldn't help it." I was getting anxious now, too.

We switched positions and soon I was on top, thrusting into her, losing myself in the feeling of being in love.

While she gazed up at me, I slid my hand between her legs, rubbing her, heightening her pleasure. I watched her, listening to the carnal sounds she made and getting a thrill from it.

I was buried deep inside her when she came. I came, too, spilling into her, in hot anticipation of the bride and groom we were destined to become.

Two days later, Tracy and I convened in the barn, hanging out with Valentine and preparing to make our relationship known. On this picturesque afternoon we would be announcing our engagement, by way of Instagram.

We'd dressed casually for the occasion; we were just being ourselves. Along with jeans and boots, I wore a plaid shirt and Tracy sported a Western blouse with an embroidered yoke and pearl snaps. Her hair was long and loose, her makeup soft and feminine.

"Are you ready?" I asked.

"Yes, absolutely." She smiled, her blue eyes twinkling.

I removed my phone from my pocket. I liked that we had control of the pictures. Of course, once we posted them, they would be picked up by news outlets and celebrity gossip sites. But Tracy and I weren't flying blind. Until we were ready to give interviews, my publicist would be making statements on our behalf. Zeke and his team were in place, too, gearing up for the fans and paparazzi who'd be waiting to catch glimpses of me and my fiancée together.

Valentine came up to the barn door, and Tracy turned to pet the filly's nose. The horse nuzzled her hand, basking in the affection.

She turned back to me, and we posed with the foal in the background. Raising Valentine was part of the life we were building, and we wanted to show her off, too.

We took a variety of shots, making sure that Tracy's ring was visible in all of them. Nothing said engaged like a big, bright diamond. I was also going to hashtag the pictures with special phrases, letting everyone know this was the woman I planned to marry. Tracy had social media accounts as well, and her following would probably skyrocket today. But we were ready for that, too. The same internet security company that monitored my accounts would also be monitoring hers from now on.

We took more pictures, enjoying the process, smiling and kissing.

Finally, we sat down to scroll through them, choosing our favorites. We narrowed it down to two: one with Valentine and one without.

"This is it," I said.

"Do it," she said.

I posted the first picture, and Tracy cuddled close to me, watching the reactions and comments pile up. With the millions of followers that I had, we would be trending at lighting speed.

"It feels good," she said.

"Totally good." Our public life together had just officially begun. There was no going back. We were a couple in every way.

Epilogue

Tracy

Three months had passed since I'd become Dash's fiancée, and on this lovely fall evening, we were hosting an engagement party.

Pine Tower was filled with friends and family. My dad was enjoying every moment. I glanced across the parlor and saw him with Spencer and Alice, the three of them chatting companionably.

Pop was strong and healthy, his recent checkup showing no signs of cancer. That gave me great peace.

Dash's mother was here, too, looking as glamorous as ever, draped in a fashionable outfit, her jewelry glittering against her skin. She'd been seeing a therapist Dash had found for her, and as far as we could tell, she was making progress. Sometimes she could still be haughty or abrasive, but she would always apologize afterward. I think she truly wanted to change. Of course, she was great in party settings. She'd helped me organize this event, making every detail shine.

She and Dash hadn't attended any family counseling sessions yet, although that was still part of the overall plan. For now, Lola was working separately on herself. As for me, I was getting stronger, too, and attending a POF support group.

I smiled in Dash's direction. He stood near the buffet, enjoying the party, socializing with our guests.

My life had changed dramatically since we'd gotten engaged. I hadn't dropped any new songs yet, but the albums I worked so hard on before—the ones that had previously bombed—were gaining momentum among Dash's fans. He was certainly proud of me. But he'd believed in me all along. I was still being cautious about the duet, though. Which I realized didn't make much sense. There was no reason for me not to sing with the wonderful man I was going to marry.

I headed toward him, and he turned and caught sight of me. He excused himself from the people he was talking to and met me halfway.

He swung me into his arms, and we kissed. He'd already told me how gorgeous I looked in my shiny gold minidress and tall black boots. He looked exceptionally handsome, too, in a finely tailored suit, his hair stylishly messy, his beard stubble wildly sexy. I could've devoured him whole.

We separated and I said, "I've been thinking… I want to write a song together and record it after we're married."

His lips tilted upward in a heart-stopping smile. "You do? For sure?"

"Yes, for sure." I grazed his cheek, running my fingers along his skin. "Our song. A love song."

He touched my face, too. "About two people who beat the odds?"

I nodded, and we kissed again, so grateful that we'd found our way back to each other.

For all time.

* * * * *